Seven years of hold

scented, gloriously long

Seven years of adm

longed to touch.

Seven years of perfectly molding her strong, athletic body to his own.

Tantalizing, torturous torment.

"I shall be a warrior queen," she'd told him, emerald eyes ablaze with fierce pride as she'd blocked and parried his blows. "A Valkyrie shield maiden, like my ancestor, Brunnhild." Agile and graceful as a dancer, she'd spun with stunning elegance and surprising force, disarming him with a glorious, gloating grin. "And I shall defend this kingdom with my sword…thanks to you."

She'd strolled across the heather blooms to pick up and return his fallen blade. And—long red hair whipping in the salty sea spray like a glorious Viking goddess—she'd kissed him, her full, sensuous lips bestowing a generous gift of gratitude.

And the promise of invigorating, intoxicating, impossible love.

L'amour impossible.

The courtly love of a chivalrous knight for a lofty lady he could never have.

So, he'd worshipped her in his young heart, suffering in silence as she honed her impressive skills and shared her secret hopes for the future as a powerful, invincible queen.

A Viking warrior queen.

A valorous Valkyrie shield maiden.

A voluptuous vixen who danced in his daring dreams.

Praise for Jennifer Ivy Walker

"I loved the world-building, the drama… fantasy settings from actual places like France, Ireland, and Britain."

~Jennifer Ibiam, Readers' Favorite

"an incredible tale of love, courage, sacrifice, and the everlasting fight between good and evil."

~Pikasho Deka, Readers' Favorite

"A wildly romantic adventure, filled with the stuff of legends."

~Author Helen Johannes

"I loved Lancelot… he's the complete package: boyish charms, loyal, and a brave knight."

~Sophia Greenwalt, Goodreads

"Filled with magic, evil, fairies, wizards, and plenty of knights and princesses, this book has a well-developed plot."

~Still Moments magazine

"Her wording is precise, lyrical, and beautiful, and character depictions are vivid and enthralling."

~Author Barbara Bettis

Winter Solstice in the Crystal Castle

by

Jennifer Ivy Walker

Christmas in the Castle Series

Jennifer Ivy Walker

Contact Information: info@thewildrosepress.com

Cover Art by *Rae Monet, Inc.*

The Wild Rose Press, Inc.
PO Box 708
Adams Basin, NY 14410-0708
Visit us at www.thewildrosepress.com

Publishing History
First Edition, 2023
Trade Paperback ISBN 978-1-5092-5138-4
Digital ISBN 978-1-5092-5139-1

Christmas in the Castle Series
Published in the United States of America

Dedication

To my daughter Candace, for your endless love, unwavering support, and heartwarming belief in wishes coming true.

Other Wild Rose Press Titles by Jennifer Ivy Walker:

The Emerald Fairy and the Dragon Knight
The Lady of the Mirrored Lake
The Wild Rose and the Sea Raven

Chapter 1

A Coveted Hand in Marriage

White-capped waves crashed upon the craggy cliff, sending a frothy spray high into the salty air as Gabrielle stood on the ramparts of *le Château de Beaufort*, gazing pensively at the turbulent surf. Sea gulls squawked, and white gannets soared in the gray, cloudy sky, the crisp saline scent of the sea calming her ragged nerves as the autumnal wind whipped her long red tresses and nipped at her stinging cheeks.

Her father, King Guillemin of Finistère, had sent for her to return home from Paris, for his poor health was rapidly declining. Enormous blisters now riddled his swollen feet, the incapacitating pain of gout making it nearly impossible for him to stand or walk. An unhealthy yellow pallor tinged his ruddy complexion and the whites of his eyes, and Gabrielle often heard him moaning in agony from inside the garderobe.

She swallowed an enormous lump of sadness as her throat constricted in sorrow.

Gabrielle knew that her father wished to see her wed before succumbing to his debilitating, inexorable illness. With the ridiculous, archaic French law—*la loi salique*—proclaiming that a woman could neither inherit a throne nor rule as queen in her own right, her father needed to arrange her royal marriage quickly. For if he died before her wedding, then King Philippe of France could order Gabrielle to marry a noble of his own choosing. Or confiscate her father's kingdom outright to aggrandize his own.

Sir Alphonse de Pontivy, the First Knight of *le Château de Beaufort* and her father's champion, interrupted her disquieting reverie. "Your father has requested your presence, Princess Gabrielle. I am here to escort you to his royal solar." The chivalrous knight removed his armored helmet and gallantly bowed his noble head, dark locks rippling in the salty spray. Sir Alphonse rose to his full regal height, secured his helmet back into place, and led Gabrielle inside the castle, down the long corridor, into the elegant antechamber where her royal father awaited, seated at a rectangular table with several nobles, all of whom stood and bowed reverently as she entered the room.

Straightening her windblown hair and smoothing her dark green velvet gown, Gabrielle inhaled deeply to compose herself. As she raised her royal regard to majestically greet her father's esteemed guests, her heart dropped at the sight of Sir Bastien de Landuc.

The exceptionally skilled horseman whom she'd watched every day during her equestrian lessons as a young princess. The magnificent Master of Horse for her father's royal stables. The most handsome man Gabrielle had ever seen.

Her legs weakened, and her mouth went dry.

Glossy brown waves tumbled to his expansive shoulders, the square jawline of his rugged face covered in dark stubble, a fine, jagged scar along one cheek enhancing his simmering brute strength. Smoldering eyes of deepest green blazed into hers like fiery emeralds, the intensity of his gaze robbing her of breath and coherent thought.

Her heart pounding, her legs trembling under her velvet robe, Gabrielle realized she was staring and forced her attention back to her father, who was making formal introductions.

"Gentlemen, may I present my daughter, the Princess Gabrielle of Finistère."

Four heads bowed humbly as her father, tightly gripping the arms of his informal throne, his face a grimace of excruciating pain, attempted a proud paternal smile as his suffering eyes stoically held hers. "Gabrielle, this is Prince Kaherdin, son of my loyal ally King Hoël of Armorique. You remember meeting him when we visited his oceanfront castle, *le Château Rose.*"

Gabrielle lowered her head politely as the dark-haired prince gallantly approached to bestow a royal kiss upon her slender hand.

"Greetings, Princess Gabrielle. It is a pleasure to see you again."

"*Enchantée,* Prince Kaherdin. Welcome to *le Château de Beaufort.*" Gabrielle smiled politely as the courteous prince returned to stand behind his chair at the royal table.

"And this is Sir Esclados le Ros, Lord of the *Château de Landuc* and father of our Master of Horse, Sir Bastien." King Guillemin gestured to a tall knight with bronze skin and jet-black hair streaked with silver, his chivalrous smile quite dashing as he bowed to greet her.

Sir Bastien inherited his father's striking looks, Gabrielle mused, as she nodded her head respectfully.

"Daughter, you have certainly heard tales of the

legendary First Knight of Camelot, Champion of King Arthur Pendragon, the High King of Britain. May I present the White Knight himself, Sir *Lancelot du Lac*."

Upon her father's introduction, a handsome knight clad in exquisite armor that gleamed like finely polished silver strode up to her, bowed gallantly, and kissed her hand with chivalrous *panache*. "*Enchanté, Votre Majesté.*" Flashing her a disarmingly charming boyish grin, the affable Sir Lancelot of the Lake returned to his position at her father's side.

"And you remember well Sir Bastien de Landuc, the Master of Horse. Not only does he possess unsurpassed equestrian skills, but he is an exceptional swordsman—second only to Sir Pontivy, my champion—as well as an unparalleled archer. Which is why I am appointing him to the prestigious position of your personal royal guard, charged with defending your life first and foremost. An unprecedented honor for a most worthy, valiant knight."

At this, Sir Bastien strode across the room and knelt at her feet, his handsome head bowed in homage. An intoxicatingly male scent of leather, pine, horses, and musk assailed Gabrielle's senses. Her stomach quivered as his deep, resonant voice strummed her like a harp. "My princess, I pledge to you my sword. My loyalty. *My life*." He took her hand and pressed warm, full lips upon it, a shiver rippling up her spine at his commanding touch. Intense, impassioned eyes held hers, and Gabrielle lost herself in the dark green depths, as verdant and mystical as a forbidden forest.

Her father's strained voice wafted across the room. "Now that introductions have been made…please, everyone, be seated." King Guillemin called to the servants waiting patiently near a side table where silver decanters glistened in the dim afternoon light. "Wine for my distinguished guests!"

As valets filled the gleaming goblets and placed them upon the carved golden oak table, Sir Bastien seated Gabrielle next to her father and took his own place at her right. Her heart pounding wildly in his magnetic presence, her palms went damp as she realized the reason for this meeting.

Her father had chosen her husband.

A crisp saline breeze floated through the enormous open windows, and the thunderous surf crashed upon the cliff far below the oceanfront castle. Gabrielle inhaled deeply, the smell of the sea and the rhythm of the pounding waves a soothing comfort as she prepared for the profound impact of his solemn announcement.

"Gabrielle, I have summoned you to join us since this matter concerns your future as my heir." King Guillemin gulped a large swallow of wine and laboriously shifted his weight to the side of his throne, wincing with the effort. "My health is rapidly declining, despite the best efforts of my gifted healer. I should like to see you married upon the winter solstice."

His once merry eyes, now dimmed with pain, held hers in a steadfast, resolute gaze. "Indeed, Daughter, it is my Yuletide wish to see you wed to a worthy monarch who will protect and provide for you after my demise. Which is why I have invited these loyal allies. To plan and organize the Yuletide Joust, in which I will award your hand in marriage to the champion."

Gabrielle stared bleakly into her goblet, her future as dark and obscure as the liquid she beheld.

I am nothing but chattel. A prize, like a warhorse. My only value lies in the land I bring as my dowry. Not in the fiery spirit that burns in my heart, nor my exceptional skill with the sword.

"Gabrielle, I am pressured by Robert Cauchon, *le Marquis de Nantes,* to wed you to his son Ugolin. But I agree with the dignitaries at this royal conference table that such a marriage would be politically disastrous, for Cauchon is closely allied with the notorious pirate Balthazar. The Marquis is most anxious for his son Ugolin to acquire my kingdom, with its countless inlets, coves, and sea caves where pirates could seize and raid incoming ships. And hide valuable contraband—such as food, wine, slaves, and gold."

The king struggled to reposition his frail body in the uncomfortable red velvet tufted throne, his voice tense and strained. "If Ugolin Cauchon were to wed you and thus become King of Finistère, then *le Traîté Maritime*—the Maritime Treaty which ensures safe passage along the Breton coast—would undoubtedly be revoked. Ugolin would thus control the Atlantic coast of France from his father's *Château de Pornic* in Nantes, at the mouth of the Loire River, all the way north to the southern shores of Britain."

Her father judiciously eyed Prince Kaherdin. "And, with his kingdom encompassing the entire northern coastline of France extending east to the shores of Armorique, Ugolin would control all shipping in the Narrow Sea. Hence, all trade with Paris."

Making King Ugolin of Finistère even more powerful than King Philippe of France, Gabrielle realized grimly.

The rich baritone of Prince Kaherdin's deep voice was a jarring counterpoint to her father's weak whisper. "We cannot allow Robert Cauchon or his son Ugolin to have sovereignty over the Breton seas. We must prevent the royal marriage which *le Marquis de Nantes* is pressuring your father to arrange." The shrewd, dark eyes of the Prince of Armorique boldly held her glum gazc.

"Although he does not threaten me overtly, for such a hostile move would alienate a potential alliance," her father explained as he drained his chalice, "Ugolin's affiliation with marauding pirates is a thinly veiled attempt to blackmail me into accepting his proposal of marriage."

His goblet raised for a servant to refill, King Guillemin quickly downed its contents before continuing. "Rather than reject his offer outright, which would anger and insult him, potentially provoking a pirate attack… I have instead decided to host a Yuletide Joust, so that another champion may win your coveted hand. Sir Lancelot and Lord Esclados—owners of the most magnificent stables in all of Bretagne—will organize the tournament on my behalf. The Yuletide Joust will take place here at *le Château de Beaufort,* beginning on the fourteenth of December, with the royal wedding and ball to be held on the sixteenth. It is my Christmas wish to see you, my precious daughter, wed to the champion. I pray that it is not Ugolin Cauchon, *le Vicomte de Nantes.*" King Guillemin raised his mug again, gulping the wine as if to drown his pain.

And sorrow.

Sir Lancelot addressed the assembled group. "On the morrow, I'll ride back to my castle—*la Joyeuse Garde*—and prepare the horses and grooms for the upcoming joust. I'll return in a few weeks with a regiment of my finest knights, to bolster your defenses,

King Guillemin. With his unscrupulous reputation, Ugolin Cauchon might very well plan a pirate attack to coincide with the tournament—to prevent anyone else from winning the princess' hand in marriage. You'll be well prepared, Your Majesty, should he try any such subterfuge." Sir Lancelot raised his goblet in tribute to her father, who nodded solemnly in grateful acknowledgement as he gulped from his own silver chalice.

Sir Lancelot is the finest knight in the Celtic realm. He will aid Sir Pontivy and Sir Bastien in my father's feeble defense. For I, as a woman, cannot. If not for la loi salique, I would be crowned queen without question. Why must the throne—which is my heritage and birthright—be given to a man?

"And I shall return to *le Château de Landuc*, in the Forest of Brocéliande, to procure additional horses for the Yuletide Joust," Lord Esclados informed her father. "I'll come back here in early December with horses, knights, and grooms. *Le Château de Beaufort* will be well guarded, Your Royal Highness, for the entire Yuletide season—during preparations for the joust, while the tournament is taking place, throughout the wedding, ball, and period of celebration. We'll ensure the safety of Princess Gabrielle and the entire castle. It will be a most joyous holiday season, Your Majesty. May your Yuletide wish to see your daughter safely wed come true."

King Guillemin smiled weakly, his arms shaking as he clutched his tufted throne. "Thank you, Lord Esclados. I am grateful for the unwavering support of all of you—my loyal, trusted allies. As we part ways, I bid you a fond farewell. Until we meet again—in three months' time."

With graceful bows and lowered heads, the distinguished guests departed from her father's royal solar, leaving Gabrielle and her personal guard Sir Bastien alone with the king. As his chamberlain Ezhvin approached to escort the ailing monarch to his royal chambers, Gabrielle's father attempted a grin and chortled, "Now you can resume the horseback riding lessons that you loved so much as a young girl. What better instructor than the Master of Horse himself? And Sir Bastien will not only enhance your impressive equestrian skills, but also protect you as well with his inimitable sword." King Guillemin gestured for her to approach so that he could kiss each of her cheeks with *la bise* of farewell. "Enjoy your ride, my daughter. It is a glorious, blustery day. Perfect for galloping across the windswept Breton moor."

With a generous paternal smile tempered by debilitating pain, Gabrielle's father clutched Ezhvin's massive arm to rise unsteadily on weakened, wobbly legs.

Gabrielle blinked back tears as she watched her once robust, burly father—descended from the renowned Viking chieftain Rollon—slowly hobble away.

"Would you care to ride, my princess?" The rich timbre of Sir Bastien's deep voice stirred her suffering soul, his expectant gaze promising an afternoon of invigorating challenge amidst the uplifting, natural beauty of the savage Breton coast.

Jubilant, ephemeral, fragile freedom.

"I would love that, Sir Bastien. Please, let's go!"

Chapter 2

L' Amour Impossible

Sir Bastien de Landuc had come to *le Château de Beaufort* as a seven-year-old page, sent by his father Lord Esclados le Ros to join his older brother Gaultier in training to become a knight, their younger sibling Cardin arriving the following autumn. For the past seventeen years, Bastien had loyally served King Guillemin in the oceanfront castle perched high on a craggy, peninsular cliff overlooking the tumultuous Atlantic Ocean. The kingdom of Finistère, in westernmost Bretagne. The region known as *Land's End.*

He'd begun as squire for Sir Alphonse de Pontivy, the First Knight of Beaufort who had been the liege lord responsible for Bastien's knighthood, his promising horsemanship, and exceptional talent with the sword.

But Bastien de Landuc owed his unparalleled equestrian skills and inimitable swordsmanship to Sir Lancelot of the Lake, the legendary First Knight of King Arthur Pendragon of Camelot.

His hero. His mentor. His friend.

Each summer, Lancelot sailed from Britain to his private French castle—*la Joyeuse Garde*—on the Élorn River in southern Bretagne, where he maintained magnificent stables, bred the finest horses, and trained the most intrepid knights in the Celtic realm. Thanks to his father's close association with Lancelot, Bastien de Landuc had spent every summer for the past ten years with the peerless knight who had instilled in him a profound love of horses, incomparable expertise in the saddle, and extraordinary prowess with the sword.

Because of his adroitness as a horseman, Bastien had been groomed to become the Master of Horse at *le Château de Beaufort.* For years, as he trained and cared for the magnificent horses in King Guillemin's royal stables, he'd watched the young princess Gabrielle develop her own impressive equestrian skills, her evident love of horses equaling his own.

Nearly every day, Bastien had ridden with the royal guards to escort Gabrielle as she galloped across the wild moors strewn with pink and purple heather, her long red tresses whipped by the wind, her beautiful face exuberant with joy. With her impetuous spirit, flaming locks, feral eyes, and fierce love of horses, she'd captured his adolescent heart.

Because of his exceptional talent in the saddle and extraordinary skill with the sword—in addition to his proximity in age to the princess—King Guillemin had selected Bastien as Gabrielle's equestrian tutor. And, since the generous king always indulged his precious, only child—he'd given in to her insistent pleas to learn the dagger, the bow, and the sword.

So, Bastien had also become her weapons instructor, honing her innate skills as he nurtured her imaginative childhood dreams.

Each morning, they would ride across the moors to a flat, open field atop the peninsular cliff shielded by thick, dense forest and the surrounding savage sea. Beginning when she was ten years old to his thirteen, he'd taught her the very skills he'd been learning as a squire.

With wooden swords and shields, he'd demonstrated lunges, strikes, and defensive blocks. He'd trained her to race her horse *Marivée* toward the target he'd created—a tall, wooden tree trunk with a strike zone area outlined in the center. Beginning with a wooden sword, she'd progressed to hitting the target with her sheathed weapon, and finally, her naked, lethal blade.

In addition to the target drills on horseback, Bastien had also taught her self-defense moves—how to break free of various strongholds as she learned a man's weaknesses—how to kick or knee the groin, strike the windpipe, gouge eye sockets, or stomp on a foot to loosen a hostile grip. He'd often wrapped his arms around her neck, as if he were an assassin, teaching her to thrust her arms up through his own, or deliver a savage blow to the ribs with her elbows as she spun to inflict a lethal slice with her sharp dagger.

He'd taught her archery, positioning her perpendicular to the target, guiding her torso into proper form, instructing her to nock and tightly draw back the bowstring, keeping her collarbone parallel with the arrow. At first, she'd been unable to hit even a close target, but after seven years of nearly daily practice, she'd developed unerring accuracy and precision.

Seven years of holding her close, inhaling her rose scented, gloriously long red hair.

Seven years of admiring the soft, porcelain skin he longed to touch.

Seven years of perfectly molding her strong, athletic body to his own.

Tantalizing, torturous, torment.

"I shall be a warrior queen," she'd told him, emerald eyes ablaze with fierce pride as she'd blocked and parried his blows. "A Valkyrie shield maiden, like my ancestor, Brunnhild." Agile and graceful as a dancer, she'd spun with stunning elegance and surprising force, disarming him with a glorious, gloating grin. "And I shall defend this kingdom with my sword…thanks to you."

She'd strolled across the heather blooms to pick up and return his fallen blade. And—long red hair whipping in the salty sea spray like a glorious Viking goddess—she'd kissed him, her full, sensuous lips bestowing a generous gift of gratitude.

And the promise of invigorating, intoxicating, impossible love.

L'amour impossible.

The courtly love of a chivalrous knight for a lofty lady he could never have.

So, he'd worshipped her in his young heart, suffering in silence as she honed her impressive skills and shared her secret hopes for the future as a powerful, invincible queen.

A Viking warrior queen.

A valorous Valkyrie shield maiden.

A voluptuous vixen who danced in his daring dreams.

Each summer, while Bastien traveled south to train with Lancelot at *la Joyeuse Garde*, Gabrielle voyaged to Paris to visit her father's aunt Béatrice, *La Duchesse de Rohan.* Four years ago, she'd been sent to live with her great-aunt among the royal courtiers residing in *le Palais de la Cité*.

To learn the proper, fastidious etiquette required of

a future French queen.

But now, with his health so precarious and rapidly declining, King Guillemin had called Gabrielle home to Finistère. So that he could arrange a royal marriage for his precious daughter before his inevitable, impending death.

It had been four long years since Bastien had last seen her. He'd since become a full-fledged knight. Master of Horse at *le Château de Beaufort*. With his brothers and fellow soldiers, he'd done his fair share of winning, wining, and wenching.

Yet—as soon as she'd entered the royal solar, her long red hair gloriously windblown, her cheeks flushed by the salty spray of the sea, her sensuous curves outlined by the alluring cling of her emerald velvet gown—Gabrielle's beauty had struck him like a blow to the gut, expending the very breath from his lungs.

His glorious Viking goddess had returned to claim him.

Heart, body, and soul.

And now, King Guillemin had appointed Bastien as Gabrielle's royal personal guard. Once again, he'd have the exquisite joy of being at her side every day. Galloping across the wild moors together. Honing her skills with the bow, dagger, and sword. Practicing self-defense. Holding her in his arms. Yearning to make her truly his.

Forced to endure her unavoidable, unbearable, unfathomable marriage to another.

Reality gripped his heart in a tight, unyielding vice.

In the stables, now preparing for their afternoon ride, her magnificent horse *Marivée* snorted as he tugged the saddle straps securely, clenching his jaw as he awaited Gabrielle's arrival.

The unbridled joy in her lilting voice was music to his sullen ears. "I cannot wait to ride again," she exhaled, affectionately stroking the muzzle of her beautiful gray Andalusian.

Marivée nickered in response, enormously pleased to be reunited with her owner.

"In Paris, the ladies of the court content themselves with embroidery, pastries, and gossip. It was stifling and suffocating. I am so glad to return to the sea." Gabrielle inhaled deeply, her eyes closed, savoring the tangy brine of the crisp, salty air.

The brisk September breeze blew a long red lock across her blissful face.

Bastien barely resisted the urge to brush it away from her soft cheek. He swallowed and spoke instead. "Our horses are ready. A royal escort awaits, to aid me in defending you as we gallop across the moor. I thought you might like to ride out to the ledge where we used to practice. Perhaps watch the ocean." He smiled softly as his eyes met hers, the green depths as enticing as her alluring velvet gown.

He lowered his gaze deferentially—a respectful, dutiful knight. Yet, fiery blood raced in his raging, rebellious veins.

"I would love that, Bastien. It's perfect. I'd like to resume my riding lessons. And weaponry training. After four years in Paris, I am completely out of practice. I want to regain my ease in the saddle. And skill with the sword. May we begin today?"

He had not expected that she'd want to practice with weapons today. With a curt nod and a brisk command to two nearby stable hands, he quickly obtained a sheath and a sword. "Of course, Your Majesty. Let me help you with the strap." As he secured the belt at her waist, a jolt of desire shot through him as he gripped the curve of her hips.

He abruptly turned away and adjusted his clothing, hoping that she had not noticed his body's ardent response.

"Thank you, Bastien. Will you please give me a boost into the saddle?"

"With pleasure, my princess." Nodding humbly, he placed her booted foot in the stirrup, wrapped his hands around her small waist, another surge rushing through him as he hoisted her high into the air.

Bastien watched with unabashed longing as she tucked the voluminous folds of her gown between her lean, lithe legs. He gulped, tamping down his yearning.

And adjusted his breeches again.

Excitement and anticipation blazed in her glorious green eyes as she looked expectantly at him.

Pulse racing, limbs shaking, desire throttling, Bastien climbed into the saddle. Swallowing forcefully, he shook his head like a stallion. And led Gabrielle, galloping across the heathered moors.

Back to the remarkable realm of their enchanted childhood.

Chapter 3

A Trinity of Mothers

The crisp green notes of pine and rowan mingled with the sweet fragrance of chamomile as Viviane harvested the yellow and white blossoms amid an early morning symphony of chirps, whistles, and trills. The *alouette* songbirds serenaded the Lady of the Lake as she carried the basket of aromatic herbs through the dense forest back to her castle, situated at the confluence of four languid lakes whose shimmering surfaces glimmered with dappled sunlight.

Le Château de Comper. The glistening castle whose pristine white limestone walls sparkled like pure, radiant crystal.

Hence the name—the *Crystal Castle.*

Where her son Lancelot would be coming home for the upcoming holiday season. To play the role of *Père Noël*. And make a little boy's greatest Yuletide wish come true.

Viviane sighed with expectant delight. *It will be a most wondrous winter solstice in the glorious Crystal Castle.*

Her solicitous valet Jacques graciously opened the ornately carved wooden door to greet l*a châtelaine* as Viviane entered the welcoming foyer. Rays of brilliant color, cast from a stained-glass transom window above the entrance, reflected off the crystals in the central chandelier onto the beeswax-scented, gleaming pinewood floors. Embroidered floral tapestries adorned the ivory plastered walls above a marble-topped table displaying a fragrant bouquet of white meadowsweet, wild angelica, and soft purple mallow flowers.

With a grateful nod to Jacques, Viviane strolled down the wide hall into the bright kitchen nook where she always prepared fresh herbs. Laying her basket upon the wooden countertop, she peered out the open window to gaze at the limpid depths of *le Lac de Diane.* The beautiful lake named for the huntress Diana, Goddess of the wilderness and the moon. Viviane smiled softly as she caressed the beloved necklace at the base of her throat. Moonstone. Diana's gem. And Viviane's sacred stone.

"I've prepared oat cakes with cinnamon and honey, and a *tarte aux mirabelles* with the last batch of our wild sweet plums. Gaston will be delighted." Sophie, Viviane's cook—who was also a talented *pâtissière*—beamed with pride as she displayed an appetizing assortment of creative confections, her merry eyes twinkling with glee.

Viviane kissed the floured, wrinkled cheek. "You, my dearest Sophie, are an absolute marvel. What would I ever do without you?"

Sophie chuckled, disappearing into the adjacent welcoming solar where Viviane would soon receive her invited guests. Amid the cheerful clatter of silverware and the clinking of glasses, Viviane returned to the chamomile blossoms to prepare a *tisane.* As she steeped the flowers in steaming water to make an exquisite herbal tea, the pounding of hooves and snorting of horses announced the arrival of her expected visitors.

Sir Esclados le Ros and his auburn-haired wife Laudine, the Lord and Lady of the *Château de Landuc*, with an entourage of a dozen armored knights, squires, and a young page of about ten years old, dismounted with hearty grins as Viviane strolled up to the edge of the forest to greet them.

"Welcome, it is wonderful to see you both! Please, come in. Sophie has outdone herself once again." Viviane kissed each of Laudine's cheeks with *la bise* of greeting as Esclados directed the knights, squires, and horses toward the awaiting grooms and adjacent manor house where they would be lodging throughout the upcoming holiday season.

His gleaming white smile offset by the deep bronze tint of his burnished skin, Esclados—nicknamed the Red Knight due to his distinctive red surcoat emblazoned with the heraldry of a golden eagle—bowed gallantly as he kissed her hand. "Viviane, you are as lovely as always. Thank you for the invitation. We bring news from King Guillemin of Finistère and look forward to your generous hospitality. And Sophie's renowned culinary delights." He chuckled heartily and introduced the young page, who approached at his gesture.

"I'd like you to meet Quentin," Esclados said affably. "An exceptional groom from my stables whom I've brought today to meet Gaston. Have Ghislaine and Gaspard arrived yet?"

"No, but I expect them very soon," Viviane replied amicably as she offered her hand in greeting to the sandy-haired, lanky youth with freckles dusted across his impish face. "*Enchantée*, Quentin. It's a pleasure to meet you. Come inside, my *pâtissière* Sophie has made some delicious treats that I'm sure you'll enjoy. Do you like *tarte aux mirabelles*?"

Quentin's twinkling eyes lit up with joy. "*Oui, madame*. It's my favorite!"

Viviane laughed softly and placed a friendly hand upon Quentin's rangy shoulder. "My dear friend Maiwenn used to make them all the time. They were her favorite, too." With a nostalgic smile, Viviane led her guests from the forest, up the beaten path, and through the carved golden oak door.

Into the splendid Crystal Castle.

"Let's wait here until Ghislaine and Gaspard arrive." Viviane gestured to a welcoming parlor where a blue velvet tufted settee and four matching chairs were arranged around a low wooden table. The enticing aromas of cinnamon and honey wafted from a tempting platter of warm oatcakes.

As her guests settled in, an amiable servant offered pewter goblets of ale to Esclados and Quentin. Viviane poured the chamomile tea she'd prepared into two ceramic mugs, handing one to Laudine. "Help yourself, Quentin. Sophie made the oatcakes especially for you and Gaston." She smiled into her cup as the boy placed one of the cinnamon flavored treats onto a plate, topped it with a generous amount of honey poured from a small jar, and bit into it with unabashed delight.

From her chair facing the window, Viviane spotted three riders emerging from the dense forest, cantering toward the château.

Dark brown curls bouncing, her deep blue cloak flapping in the autumn breeze, Ghislaine was flanked by her woodcutter husband Gaspard and their seven-year-old son, Gaston. The young boy who idolized Sir

Lancelot of the Lake. The unsuspecting child whose greatest Yuletide wish would soon come true.

Beyond his wildest dreams.

Viviane's heart fluttered in eager anticipation of the most wondrous winter solstice yet in her sparkling Crystal Castle.

"Here they are!" she exclaimed exuberantly, rising from her chair as the valet Jacques opened the entrance door to greet the invited guests.

Amid the red and gold leaves rustling across the grassy courtyard in front of the castle, the trio of visitors dismounted, handing the horses' reins to stable hands, as Viviane hurried down the path and hugged her smiling friends. "Welcome, everyone!" Wrapping Gaston in an affectionate embrace, she greeted him with la *bise* and whispered in his ear, "You're just in time for Sophie's oatcakes. And she even made *tarte aux mirabelles!"*

Eyes as blue as *le Lac de Diane* widened in wonder. "*Tarte aux mirabelles?* My favorite!" Gaston hugged her waist, his dark brown locks shining in the luxuriant morning light.

Viviane's heart flooded with joy. "Go on ahead. Sophie's in the parlor with a boy named Quentin. He's a squire, about your age. Sir Esclados brought him today, so you'd have someone to practice sword fighting with. We'll be along in just a moment."

His strong, sturdy legs churning up the beaten path, Gaston bolted toward the tempting treats and the unexpected delight of a seasoned sparring partner.

Viviane linked her elbow in Ghislaine's offered arm and led her laughing guests into *le Château de Comper*.

In the parlor, Gaston was gobbling an oatcake laden with honey as Esclados, Laudine, and the squire Quentin stood to greet the new arrivals.

Ghislaine and Laudine, close friends who often visited Viviane, kissed on the cheeks as their husbands shook hands.

Esclados introduced the older boy to Gaston's parents. "This is Quentin, a page and stable groom from my *Château de Landuc*. I thought Gaston might enjoy a bit of training from an experienced swordsman."

Quentin's chest puffed out with pride as he grinned from ear to ear, enormously pleased at the praise from the prestigious Red Knight.

An awestruck Gaston gazed at Quentin, respect and admiration blazing in his bright blue eyes.

A plump, matronly figure in a white linen apron and close-fitting bonnet appeared in the doorway. "*Bonjour, messieurs dames.* Everything is ready. Please, follow me. Right this way." Sophie's round cheeks crinkled in a welcoming grin as she ushered the guests from the parlor into the adjacent banquet room.

Dappled sunlight filtered from the dense trees surrounding the castle, through a large open window, onto a rectangular table where pitchers of ale and mead were placed among platters of oat wafers, almond cakes, and two magnificent *tarte aux mirabelles*. The sweet aromas of cinnamon, honey, almonds, and wild plums merged with the fresh herbal fragrance of chamomile from a steaming teapot in the center of the appetizing array.

As her guests were seated, the *domestique* Odille joined Sophie in serving chalices of mead for the men and mugs of watered ale for the boys while Viviane poured *tisane* for her female guests and herself. Everyone dug in, raving about the delicious treats—

especially the wild plum tarts.

Soon, the joyful shouts of the boys, eager to escape the confines of the castle and practice swordsmanship with wooden weapons, carried into the banquet hall. “I am Sir Lancelot of the Lake, First Knight of King Arthur Pendragon!” Gaston cried, his jubilant voice floating on the late September wind. “*En garde*!”

As the mock battle commenced, Viviane laughed softly and remarked, “Gaston will be ecstatic this winter solstice. He has no idea that he’ll not only get to meet his hero Lancelot, but that he’ll be traveling to Camelot, as a personal squire for my magnanimous son. I can’t wait to see Gaston’s eyes light up with Yuletide joy when he meets his hero—and learns that he will one day become a Knight of the Round Table, too!” She sipped her chamomile tisane, its comforting heat as warm as the glow in her happy heart.

Viviane glanced at Ghislaine, whose limpid eyes were brimming. With tears of joy, no doubt, for her son Gaston would be exuberantly happy to become the personal squire of Lancelot—the most reputed knight in the entire Celtic realm. Yet, Viviane knew that Ghislaine’s tears were also of despair, for her beloved son would soon be leaving her maternal arms to venture off to Britain. To a distant land, far from the familiar French forest where she and Gaspard—the middle-aged couple who had tried vainly for twenty years to conceive a child—had adopted and raised him in the humble stone cottage with the straw thatched roof.

Memories flooded Viviane.

The poor young priestess, desperate to hide her impossible pregnancy. The childless couple yearning for a babe of their own.

Viviane had arranged it all.

She'd brought the frantic expectant mother to Ghislaine's cottage, where the girl had remained hidden throughout her pregnancy. Laudine—an experienced, capable midwife—had delivered the infant and cared for the young mother for the first few months as she nursed the babe that she loved with every fiber of her being but could not possibly keep.

And, when the infant Gaston was old enough to eat gruel and take milk from a cup—the despairing, devastated, doomed mother relinquished her cherished son to Ghislaine and Gaspard.

With the sacred promise to forever keep her secret and never reveal the painful truth.

And so, they had.

Ghislaine's quavering voice brought Viviane back to the present. "Now that he is seven years old—the age when boys enter training to become a knight—we had thought of sending Gaston to Finistère. To squire for one of your three sons, Laudine." Ghislaine sipped her tisane and gazed out the window, watching the sparring boys who would one day become valiant knights. "It seemed a logical choice…for Gaston to serve King Guillemin in *le Château de Beaufort.*" Anguish and elation warred in her impassioned eyes. "But, for him to have the opportunity to train with the legendary Lancelot...to travel to Camelot and become a Knight of the Round Table of King Arthur Pendragon…" Her hand shook violently, *tisane* spilling down her chalice as tears spilled down her cheeks. "His greatest Yuletide wish will indeed come true." Ghislaine held Viviane's gaze with gratitude, guilt, and grief. "But it will be so hard to let him go…" she buried her face in her hands, succumbing to smothering sobs.

Gaspard wrapped his tree trunk arms around his heartbroken wife, cradling her against his solid chest. "Shhh…it will be fine. He'll come back to Bretagne every summer with Lancelot to train at *la Joyeuse Garde*. We'll see him often, my love. And he will become as fine a knight as his mentor. Imagine—our son Gaston, a Knight of King Arthur's Round Table!" The deep timbre of his voice soothing as a mellow harp, he rocked her, showering her dark curls with comforting kisses, infusing his wife with supportive strength and shared parental pride.

Ghislaine lifted her tear-stained face. "You're right. I must think of Gaston and how much this will mean to him. It is truly the chance of a lifetime." With a crumpled smile, she whispered to Viviane, "Thank you. For my beloved son… and for this extraordinary opportunity. I am forever grateful." She reached across the table and affectionately grasped Viviane's hand.

The Lady of the Lake squeezed it firmly in return.

Viviane spoke to Esclados. "You mentioned that you bring news from King Guillemin of Finistère. Is everything all right with your three sons?"

"Yes, indeed—they all fare well, each one a respected knight of *le Château de Beaufort.* Our son Bastien, as you know, is the king's eminent Master of Horse. But he has recently received an additional, most prestigious title. Now that the Princess Gabrielle has been called home from Paris—due to her father's poor health—Bastien has been appointed as her personal royal guard."

"Congratulations. What an exceptional honor!" Viviane clasped Esclados' calloused hand and beamed with genuine pleasure and affection.

"He'll also resume the equestrian lessons he used to give her as a young girl." Laudine sipped her *tisane*, her amber eyes glistening in the morning light. "Perhaps even the intensive training that so scandalized the courtiers of Paris, shocked that a pretty princess would want to wield a weapon." A sly grin spread across her bemused face. "They could never imagine a mere woman as a warrior. But I remember Bastien saying that Gabrielle had exceptional skill in the saddle. With a bow and arrow. And especially with the sword."

Esclados took a large gulp of mead and swiped a swarthy hand across his trimmed beard, his eyebrows lowering into a pensive frown. "King Guillemin is anxious to see his daughter wed. With his health rapidly declining, he must arrange a royal wedding as soon as possible." He leaned back in his chair, crossing chiseled arms against his broad chest. "The Marquis de Nantes, Robert Cauchon, is pressuring the king to marry Gabrielle to his son Ugolin. But Cauchon is closely allied with the infamous pirate Balthazar. If his son were to marry Gabrielle and become the King of Finistère, Cauchon and Ugolin would control all shipping on the Breton seas, from the Loire River to the mouth of the Seine. King Guillemin cannot allow that to happen. Which is why he is hosting a Yuletide Joust, with Gabrielle's hand in marriage offered to the champion."

Laudine leaned forward expectantly, her voice a breathless whisper. "Lancelot and Esclados, with their magnificent stables, will arrange and implement the joust, providing the *destriers* for the tournament. Which Bastien will oversee, in his role as Master of Horse. The Yuletide Joust will take place on the fourteenth of

December, with three days of celebration, culminating in the royal wedding on the sixteenth. Pray that it is not Ugolin Cauchon who wins Princess Gabrielle's coveted hand."

Two eager, grimy faces appeared in the doorway. Gaston regarded his father, an irresistible plea in his big blue eyes. "Can we please practice with you?"

Gaspard grinned at Esclados as he rose to his full, towering height. "Let's leave our wives to chat with our amiable hostess, while you and I get a few of the knights to train with the boys."

"Sounds good. *Allons-y*. Let's go." The Red Knight stood, stretched out his strong back, and strapped on his superb Spanish sword. He winked at his wife, white teeth gleaming against his dark, handsome face. "We'll leave you—this lovely trinity of mothers—to plan the upcoming winter solstice." He glanced at Gaston, his eyes full of merry mirth. "I wonder what *Le Père Noël* will bring this Christmas?"

As the chuckling men departed with exuberant boys whooping with glee, Viviane smiled contentedly at Laudine. "With Gabrielle's wedding following the Yuletide Joust, our sons will be home just in time for the winter solstice." She reached across the table to squeeze Ghislaine's trembling hand. "For my son to make your son's Yuletide wish come true."

A lone tear trickled down Ghislaine's smiling cheek. "Gaston will be overjoyed. I cannot wait to see his astonished face when he meets the great Lancelot of the Lake." She dried her eyes, inhaled deeply, and sipped her *tisane*. She turned to Laudine. "Will all three of your sons be home for the holidays?"

"I truly hope so. I do expect Gaultier. And Cardin,

our youngest—with his betrothed, the Lady Charlotte of Saint-Renan." Laudine sipped her herbal tea and sighed. "But, with Bastien now serving as personal royal guard to Gabrielle, I doubt that he will be able to leave the princess he is sworn to protect." She gazed pensively into her *tisane*. "Of all my three sons, he's the one I worry about most. Gaultier, as our oldest, will inherit *le Château de Landuc.* And Charlotte's dowry includes land and a small castle in western Bretagne, close enough for Cardin to remain in loyal service to King Guillemin while raising a family of his own. But Bastien, as our middle son, will inherit neither land nor title. And I fear that he may never marry. For I believe my chivalrous, gallant son lost his heart long ago."

Sorrow shone in her expressive amber eyes as she held Viviane's gaze.

"To the feisty, fiery princess. Gabrielle of Finistère."

Chapter 4

The Viking Princess of Finistère

He loved watching her long red hair billow in the briny wind, sheathed sword strapped at her slender hip, black cloak unfurling like the enormous swan wings of a Valkyrie shield maiden.

Marivée, her fleet footed gray Andalusian, flew across the heathered moors, the horse's incredible speed a sheer, thrilling delight to the free spirited, flame haired, fire hearted Gabrielle.

Every morning, they zigzagged through the dense woods, racing to the expansive plateau on the peninsular clifftop where—a dozen royal knights standing guard at the edge of the forest—Bastien honed the equestrian and weaponry skills of his princess protégée.

She'd surpassed her previous expertise in the saddle and accuracy with the bow and arrow, yet struggled to regain her precision with the blade. So, after riding and archery, they focused on self-defense moves with the dagger. And offensive attacks with the sword.

Holding her against him as she struggled to break free was agonizing, torturous pleasure. Her intoxicating scent, the feel of her body moving against his, the unbearable desire building more each day…the only way he was able to maintain control was by withdrawing into a sullen, solitary soldier focused solely on battle.

"Extend your arm like this, to parry my downward diagonal cut." He stood behind her, guiding her weapon as he explained the defensive technique. "Block the blow and launch into your own attack." Bastien raised her arm to simulate absorbing a strike, pulling her into a sidestep and swirling into a counterattack as she parried his opposing sword. "Now, control the flow and force me back."

Breathless with excitement, she blocked his strike, deftly twirling her body and blade, disarming him in a sudden, surprising surge of strength.

Long red tresses whipping wildly in the wind, a triumphant smile illuminating her sun kissed cheeks, she reveled in the glorious thrill of victory.

His Viking Princess of Finistère.

"It's exhilarating!" she cried exuberantly, her dark green eyes ablaze. "I've regained my strength and skill… enough to disarm my chivalrous royal guard." She bent to retrieve his weapon, handing it to him as he sheathed the returned blade. "Thank you for allowing me that. I know it was a gift to restore my pride. Perhaps one day…I'll be able to do it on my own."

She gazed out at the sea and inhaled deeply, then whirled toward him with an impish grin. "I'd love to walk on the beach. Let's ride up ahead, through the forest. We can tether the horses and leave them with the guards at the edge of the cliff, while we follow the path down to the shore. It's such a beautiful day, I have no desire to return to the dismal castle and my dreary duties as princess. Will you escort me, my loyal royal guard?" She laughed freely, raced to her magnificent gray horse, and slid effortlessly into the saddle, as if she had been born to ride across the wild, windswept moors of the craggy Breton coast.

Bastien dashed after her, mounted his robust stallion Drach, and barked commands to the awaiting royal guards. Soon, he was galloping through the dense forest in pursuit of the impetuous princess, followed by a dozen armored knights of *le Château de Beaufort.*

They arrived at a clearing near the edge of the woods on top of the precipice overlooking the expansive sea. A narrow path led from the forested ledge down to a secluded, sandy shore sheltered by the protective jutting curve of the jagged, rocky cliff.

Tethering the horses to graze with the dozen royal guards who dismounted to rest their chargers, Bastien took Gabrielle's hand and led her down the long, narrow, winding path to the white sandy shore of the beach far below.

Pounding waves crashed against the rocky outcrop, the turbulent surf reduced to a gentle inlet which lapped upon the sandy shore. Fluffy clouds scattered across the cerulean sky, seagulls squawking in the saline spray as Gabrielle sat down upon a large rock.

"Please, allow me." Bastien unlaced and removed her pointed leather boots, sitting beside her to remove his own.

She stood and stretched, extending her arms above her head. Eyes closed, she raised her face to the sky, as if savoring the warmth of the mild, late autumn sun. "The sun feels good," she hummed, "and I love the crisp, cleansing scent of the sea." Lowering her beautiful, blissful face, she beamed at him.

And took his breath away.

"Look!" she cried, pointing toward the curved cliff. "There's a sea cave up ahead. Let's explore!"

Drawing his sword, Bastien insisted on inspecting the cave before allowing Gabrielle to enter.

Inside the limestone grotto, which was burrowed into the curved face of the cliff, sand covered one side of the cave floor, forming a path—with seawater flowing along the other wall into a brilliant turquoise pool. The back of the cave, which curved deeper into the foundation of the bluff, was dry sand and solid rock, the hollow walls echoing and reverberating the roar of the pounding surf.

"This is magical!" Gabrielle exuded when Bastien beckoned her to enter and join him. Arms extending out from her sides, she spun in a dance of delight as she absorbed the astonishing raw beauty of the hidden sea cave. Pearlescent walls, laden with moisture, glistened and reflected the aqua luminescence of the pool like sparkling, glittering gems.

Bastien ventured into the dark, twisting tunnel as Gabrielle walked up behind him. "There's a passage here, leading beyond the back wall. It curves to the left—deeper into the cliff."

"Let's follow and see where it leads." Her eyes were wide with wonder, her breath hitching with excitement.

"It's too dark without a torch. We'll come back tomorrow. I'll bring one to light the way."

"An exciting adventure. I cannot wait!" Gabrielle threw her arms around his neck and exuberantly kissed his cheek.

Her scent, her touch, her full lips… Bastien's body surged in response, his limbs shaking with want and need. He retreated abruptly from her embrace and spun away, scorched by the flames of desire. "We must head back now. It's time to return to the castle. Come, my princess."

Was that hurt he glimpsed in her downcast eyes? He swallowed a sorrowful lump of guilt. She would soon be wedded to another man. She could never be his. Scowling at himself for his undeniable, unchivalrous lust, he gallantly led his princess out of the hidden cave.

They walked in silence across the secluded beach, back to the stone where he seated her and brushed the sand from her bare feet. As he gripped her ankle, her gown fell away, revealing a long, lithe white leg. Painful, throbbing desire forced him to step back and adjust his braies as he reached for her leather boots.

She looked up at him, her inquisitive eyes filled with sadness and confusion. "Is something wrong, Sir Bastien? You seem angry. Have I displeased you?"

Not you, my princess. Never you. I'm angry at myself for the impossible yearning which sickens my soul. "No, not at all, Your Majesty. Quite the contrary. I am merely preoccupied with the many duties that await me this afternoon. That is all." He forced a polite smile as he tamped down his shameful lust. Swiftly donning his own boots, he extended a chivalrous hand to help Gabrielle to her feet.

And escorted his beautiful princess up the path to the forested ledge where their horses and royal guards awaited.

****

"It is most unbecoming behavior for a future queen."

"Indeed, Béatrice, the entire Parisian court is ablaze with scandal. Princess Gabrielle, galivanting across the moors like a heathen. Bow and arrows strapped to her back, a sword sheathed at her hip. It is absolutely deplorable and utterly unacceptable. You must stop it immediately."

Gabrielle overheard the scathing remarks as she approached the royal solar to greet her great-aunt's guests who had just arrived from Paris, ostensibly for a friendly visit. But Gabrielle knew the real reason the vicious vipers were here.

To spread malicious gossip with venomous, vicarious delight.

"Ah, there you are, my dear," Béatrice cooed as Gabrielle strolled across the sunlit parlor to kiss her great-aunt's cheeks. A familiar spark of rebellious spunk blazed in those deep brown eyes. "You remember my friend Agnès, *la Marquise de Josselin*."

Gabrielle nodded politely to the plump, matronly marquise whose powdery white face and pomaded pink cheeks were pinched with haughty disdain. "*Enchantée, Madame la Marquise*."

"And Clothilde, *la Vicomtesse de Vannes*."

The gnarled knuckles and claw like nails evoked the image of a shrewish harpy as Gabrielle dutifully kissed the extended hand under the gaunt glower of the wiry witch. "It is a pleasure to see you again, *Madame la Vicomtesse*."

A rotund woman with a flushed face and sparse white curls—her ample rolls of flesh straining at the seams of her tight blue gown—gawked at Gabrielle with undisguised contempt, as if she were a slug slithering up the petals of a perfect pink rose.

"And Françoise, *la Comtesse de Ploudry*." Her great-aunt presented the pompous noble as Gabrielle bowed slightly in polite *obéisance*. "They have come to spend a few days near the sea in our lovely *Château de Beaufort.*" Béatrice gestured to a servant, who placed an appetizing platter of French pastries upon the low table as she served steaming cups of *tisane* to the pampered guests.

Gabrielle took her seat at her great-aunt's side, already desperate to escape the stifling, suffocating atmosphere of the Parisian court which aways smothered her soul. She smiled at the timid servant, accepting the proffered cup of herbal tea, grateful for the temporary distraction.

No sooner had she taken a sip than the onslaught of insults began.

"Your father the king is most anxious to see you wed, Gabrielle. I must agree, you sorely need a husband. A strong-willed man to control your impetuous spirit. It is positively improper for a princess to cavort with soldiers and wield weapons like a man." Her thin lips curling into a downward smirk of disapproval, the harsh rasp of the venomous voice scraped up Gabrielle's spine like the sharp claws of the *vicomtesse.*

"Ugolin Cauchon will not tolerate such wanton behavior in his royal wife." The powdered marquise chuckled cruelly. "He is nicknamed *Ugolin le Clou*—for he is hard as a nail. Ruthless, merciless, and relentless." Beady black eyes glinted with malicious glee as *la Marquise de Josselin* beheld Gabrielle, savoring the sting of her venom. "He might very well lock you in a tower, to *curb your wicked ways*."

As if to defend her beleaguered great-niece, Béatrice remarked affably, "Perhaps another will win Gabrielle's hand. After all, there are many potential suitors who might excel in the joust." Encouragement shone in her aunt's kind eyes as she shot Gabrielle an uplifting, hopeful gaze.

"*Ugolin le Clou* would never concede to a loss. If he can't win Gabrielle's hand in the Yuletide Joust, he'll force King Philippe to order the marriage, by threatening to halt all shipments to Paris." The harpy sipped her tea, a sadistic grin spreading across her sunken, sinister face. "Despite *le Traîté Maritime,* Ugolin and his father, Robert Cauchon, control the Breton seas." Greed glimmered in her garish gaze. "If Ugolin becomes King of Finistère, he will control all shipments to Paris, and we…" she crooned to the carrion-loving crones at her side, "will have the finest jewels, laces, and gowns. As well as the most sumptuous, decadent spices and silks imported from the Orient. Just imagine… our royal courts of Bretagne would exceed King Philippe's in Paris!"

The trio of blistering biddies tittered with titillation.

I must escape. I'll feign illness and retreat to my room. I'd rather be confined to my royal chambers than subject myself to this slow torture.

Gabrielle raised her arm, placing it against her forehead, and emitted a soft moan. "I'm dreadfully sorry, *Tante Béatrice*, but I'm feeling quite ill. I shall retire now…and leave you fine ladies to have a lovely chat." She rose unsteadily to her feet and kissed her great-aunt's cheek. With a polite curtsey and a formal farewell, she extricated herself from their caustic, contaminating company.

Alone in her room, she gazed out the window at the turbulent sea crashing against the cliff far below. *Tomorrow, Bastien and I will explore the cave. A thrilling adventure…and the chance to be alone with him again.*

She envisioned his brooding, handsome face. The

rugged, bristled chin. The thin, jagged scar. Brute strength seethed from his every pore. Solitary and sullen. Angry and withdrawn. Impossibly irresistible.

Today, when they'd discovered the hidden tunnel in the cave, she'd kissed his cheek with joy. And he had recoiled, as if scorched.

Or repulsed.

And yet… she swore that she'd seen passion blaze in his deep green gaze. The smoldering stare that bore right into her soul.

How she longed to feel his sinewy arms wrapped around her. To taste his full, luscious lips. To feel the length of his hardened body pressed against hers…

Perhaps he loved another. He might very well be betrothed to one of the ladies of the court.

She'd find out tomorrow. He was her personal guard, after all. She'd simply ask him.

And pray that the answer was no.

Because, by the Goddess…she wanted him for herself.

Chapter 5

A Secret Tunnel

The next day, after equestrian lessons, archery practice, self-defense tactics and a strenuous training session with the sword, Bastien and Gabrielle returned to the sea cave hidden in the curve of the cliff.

He led her to the back of the cave where a tunnel, not visible from the entrance of the grotto, veered to the left. Lighting the torch he'd brought and unsheathing his sword, he led Gabrielle—who drew her blade as well—into the dark, mysterious passageway.

Rich, earthy loam and the pine scent of the forest permeated the limestone walls as they followed the narrow, twisting tunnel which led deep into the foundation of the cliff at a steadily upward incline. Although there was enough width for the two of them to walk abreast, Bastien led the way, insisting on protecting his princess.

They encountered no animals or intruders, just tangled roots overhead, as if they were traveling beneath the forest. After a while, the incline of the path became quite steep, and Gabrielle sheathed her sword to accept Bastien's helping hand while she hoisted the long hem of her gown with her other.

To their mutual surprise, they arrived at an impasse where a metal door appeared in the roof of the cave above them.

He handed her the torch and sheathed his sword. “Stay here while I try to open it.” Climbing up the side embankment of the walled impasse, Bastien stood, braced himself, and—arms overhead—pushed open the trapdoor. “Please pass me the torch, so I can see inside.” With the flame that she handed him, he peered into the opening of the entrance overhead. “I can’t believe it…” he gasped, looking down at her on the floor below. “This leads into the castle!” Returning the torch to her so that he could use both arms, he pulled himself up and looked down at her from the hole above her head. “This is the bottom of the keep. In the foundation of the castle. Pass me the torch, and I’ll pull you up.”

On her knees, she climbed up the side of the loamy embankment, stood, and gripped the sides of the hole above her head. As she pulled herself up, Bastien clasped one arm, guiding her into the cavernous chamber. She rose to her feet, dusted the dirt from her gown, and took in her surroundings.

They were inside a storage area where crates of goods were stacked along the stone walls at the base of a set of stairs extending up into the castle.

Bastien climbed the steps leading to the heavy metal door and attempted to open it, but it was locked from within. “When we return to the castle, we’ll come down here and open this door. What an amazing discovery—a means of escape, should we ever need it.” He grinned at Gabrielle, whose emerald eyes blazed in the torchlight.

He slid through the trapdoor, back down into the tunnel, and accepted the torch, which he stuck firmly into the ground at his side. As she lowered her legs through the opening, he clasped her waist and eased her to the ground. Closing the trapdoor overhead, he unsheathed his sword, picked up the torch, and led Gabrielle through the dark tunnel, back toward the cave.

As they followed the meandering path, Gabrielle pointed to another passageway, leading away from the castle in a different direction. "Bastien, look! Another tunnel."

He held the torch to illuminate the path, which led away from the beach, deeper into the cliff.

"Can we follow it?" she asked breathlessly, her eyes wide with wonder.

Long red tresses cascading to her waist, smudges of grime on her eager face, her hands clasped together in anticipatory delight, she melted his hardened heart. And stirred his savage soul.

"If it pleases you, of course. But I'll lead the way."

Her dazzling smile took his breath away.

Once again, the path led in an increasingly steep incline, with thick roots overhead and the unmistakable pine scent of the forest. The dark tunnel twisted and turned, leading deeper into the base of the cliff, emptying at last into a vast cave which exited into a dense forest.

Bastien led Gabrielle out of the cavern and into the thick woods. At the sight of the familiar lake, his jaw dropped in astonishment. "That's *le Lac de Poulinoc*, where we squires used to swim and fish. My brothers and I used to hunt in this forest. We're behind the castle… about a half mile to the east." Grinning at the discovery, he led her toward the edge of the lake where rays of the afternoon sun reflected on the rippled, shimmering surface, reveling in the sheer delight on her beaming, incredulous face.

"We've found a secret passage from the castle to the

beach. And another leading into these woods." She walked up to him, her eyes aglow, her face alit with pleasure. "Thank you so much, Bastien. For this adventure. For this taste of freedom—something I never have."

Golden sunlight glittered in her deep green eyes like facets of rare emeralds. "I shall always treasure this day, this discovery. This secret we share, you and I." She placed her slender white hand over his galloping heart and stood on tiptoes to kiss his scarred cheek. Her luxurious red hair smelled of roses, her lush lips so full and soft. His body throbbed; he ached to take her in his arms. To devour her lips, caress her porcelain skin…claim her as his own.

Instead, he bowed his head respectfully and backed away, tamping down his impossible desire. "I am pleased that you enjoyed our adventure, my lady. But we must return to the castle."

"Could we come here again? I would love to practice archery in these woods."

"If that is your wish. I'll arrange for the guards to accompany us."

"No…then I'll be the royal princess again, under watchful, dutiful eyes. I want to leave that all behind—at least for a few hours. To experience the glorious thrill of freedom." She glanced longingly at the lake. "Never before have I had the chance to swim in a lake. I wish it were summertime…"

I am grateful that it is not, for if I were to swim with you...with the gown clinging to your long, lithe body, your glorious hair floating on the gentle waves...It would be agonizing, unbearable torture.

"Could we please come here tomorrow? Just you

and I?" Her large, limpid eyes imploring, he drowned in their emerald depths.

"Of course, Your Majesty. I am at your service. Always." He bent at the waist in noble *obéisance*. "But for now, we must return to the castle."

****

"Come with us, Bastien. Sir Pontivy is guarding the princess tonight, and you have the evening free. A few of the knights are going to *La Galinette*—we'll eat our fill of *moules,* drink some fine mead, find a willing tavern wench. C'mon, it'll do you good to tumble a pretty lass." Gaultier grinned as he belted his sword, a lusty glint dancing in his dark, mischievous eyes.

Several knights lingered near the castle door, waiting for Gaultier to join them.

"Not tonight. I need to check on the horses. Go on without me. And have a good time." Bastien heartily clasped his older brother's shoulder as he exited the castle. Heading toward the stables, he chuckled softly. With his dashing good looks and chivalrous charm, Gaultier was immensely popular with the ladies.

But Bastien had no desire to bed a comely tavern wench.

He yearned for the fiery, flame-haired Gabrielle.

His Viking Princess of Finistère.

****

The cold autumn breeze flushed her cheeks and rustled her hair, the tangy scent of pine filling the crisp air amid the morning trill of larks and finches. "Hold your body like this," Bastien said softly, positioning Gabrielle perpendicular to the tree trunk he'd selected as a target. As he placed his hands on her hips to align them correctly, his body thickened and throbbed as he imagined positioning them into an upward tilt to welcome and receive him.

Shaking with desire, struggling to maintain his composure, he wrapped his arms around her to nock and tightly draw back the bowstring. When his hand grazed the swell of her breast, he brusquely stepped back with a guttural grunt. He adjusted his breeches, tossed his head back, and focused on the target, trying to distract his raging thoughts and calm his racing heart. Inhaling deeply, he sighed, "Perfect… now release."

With a loud *thwack,* her arrow struck the target. She twirled toward him, her beautiful face alight with glee. "I did it! I hit the center. That's the very first time." In a swirl of green velvet, she raced to the tree and withdrew her arrows, dashing back to join him at the starting point. "I want to do it again. And practice here every day. Until I can hit the target without fail."

And so, every day for the month of November, after galloping across the moors, practicing self-defense with her dagger, and honing her skills with the sword, Bastien helped Gabrielle develop precision and accuracy with her bow.

Fueling the scorching, smoldering flames of his impossible, infernal desire.

One afternoon after intensive training, as they tethered the horses at the top of the forested ledge, preparing to walk down onto the beach, Gabrielle removed a bag from Marivée's saddle. "I've brought some food for us to share by the lake. I thought it would be nice to relax a bit after archery practice. Please tell the guards that we'll be longer than usual today."

His mouth went dry, and his stomach dropped.

Bastien strode briskly over to the guards, informing

them that the princess wished to spend more time today along the shore. With orders for the knights to remain with the horses, he quickly rejoined Gabrielle, slung her bag over his shoulder, and led her down the path to the beach.

Into their secret cave.

****

Gabrielle followed Bastien through the dark tunnel, her thoughts and emotions blazing and flickering like the torch flame.

She was inordinately proud of her achievements. She'd become a truly exceptional rider who had mastered not only the art of self-defense, but who could also wield and hurl a dagger with lethal precision. She'd honed her impressive skill with the sword and had greatly improved her accuracy with the bow and arrow.

Yet, none of these stunning accomplishments really mattered.

Because, in two short weeks, the champion of the Yuletide Joust would win her hand. And Gabrielle's freedom would disappear. Just like her foolish childhood dreams of becoming a valorous, victorious Valkyrie. A Viking warrior queen like her ancestor Brunnhild.

Instead—she'd be given away, like a prize. Denied her right to the throne. Forced to surrender her kingdom—and her body—to a stranger.

Because of a ridiculous, archaic French law—*la loi salique.*

Despair and impotent rage blazed in her fiery heart.

So, she had decided to act. To savor the ephemeral, exquisite taste of freedom.

Before it was taken away.

Although she knew perfectly well how to nock the

arrow and draw back the bowstring, she always asked for Bastien's assistance. Because she loved the feel of his arms around her. The intoxicating male scent of leather, pine, fresh sweat, and horses. The bristle of dark stubble against her cheek, the hardened length of his body against hers.

Today she would ask him. He just had to say yes.

"Please put it over there," she said cheerfully, indicating a spot on the cloth she had just spread atop the decaying leaves and earthy loam near the edge of the lake.

Bastien placed the woven basket at the corner of the woolen blanket.

"I've brought bread, cheese, and fruit," she announced, kneeling onto the cloth to unpack the supplies. "Please, sit here beside me, and pour us some wine."

A cold breeze wafted the fresh tang of the lake and the clean scent of pine, the pale winter sun filtering through the rustling leaves. Bastien handed her a goblet and sat down at her side.

She accepted the pewter chalice with a smile, swallowing a large gulp to calm her nerves. The rich, earthy flavor lingered on her tongue. As they shared the fresh grapes, nutty bread, and sharp cheese, Gabrielle mustered the courage to voice her request.

"Bastien…Lancelot will be arriving next week, with an entourage of knights, stable hands, horses, and grooms. As will your father, Sir Esclados, bringing the magnificent *destriers* from *le Château de Landuc*." Her finger traced the rim of her goblet as she stared into the dark red depths.

Gabrielle raised her eyes to meet his. "In two weeks,

at the Yuletide Joust, I will be given away. A prize, like a bag of silver or a parcel of land. A trophy for the champion who wins my hand." Unwanted tears brimmed, distorting his handsome, impassioned face. "I have precious few days of freedom left, and I want to savor every moment."

She wiped her eyes and drained her goblet, the liquid warmth fueling her courage. "I'd like very much to go into the village, disguised as a peasant. I want to eat roast boar and drink goblets of ale. Dance to a lively fiddle and laugh with unabashed joy. Enjoy my freedom…before it is taken away." She implored him with her eyes, glimpsing in his fiery green gaze an array of conflicting emotions.

Chivalrous honor. Unbridled passion. Duty and obligation.

"I can borrow a homespun gown that the kitchen servants wear. Hide my hair under a bonnet. No one will know it's me." Raising onto her knees, she clutched his hand, grasping at her last chance of liberty. "Will you please grant my wish…and take me into town? That I might taste the exquisite flavor of freedom before it is gone?"

Haunted, hungry eyes blazed into hers. Bastien raised her hand to his soft, full lips, a shiver of pleasure rippling down her arm, a warm glow igniting in her loins. "I will do anything you ask of me. Anything to please you. Of course, I will grant your wish."

His thumb traced her fingers as he stared pensively at her hand, raising his dark green gaze which sparkled in the late morning light. "But we must ride different horses, for our own would be easily recognized." Still holding her hand, he looked out at the lake, his brows furrowed in concentration. "Tonight, at dinner time, tell your attendants that you're ill and wish to retire early. Leave instructions that you must not be disturbed. Dress like a chambermaid and meet me in the kitchen pantry. We'll slip down into the buttery where the barrels of ale are stored and take the exit near the stables. I'll have two horses saddled and waiting for us."

She sprung to her feet, pulling him to a stand before her. With a squeal of delight, she flung her arms around his neck and kissed his stubbled cheek. "Thank you, Bastien! I cannot wait!"

In his conflicted gaze, Gabrielle glimpsed wild, exuberant joy and desperate, overwhelming guilt.

Seeming to struggle with contradictory emotions, he silently helped her repack the basket.

Reenter the secret cave.

And—as if condemned by fate—return stoically to the *château.*

Chapter 6

A Trio of Yuletide Wishes

An early December chill nipped at Viviane's cheeks, the dark, cloudy sky hinting at snow as she carried an armful of evergreen boughs and pine branches back toward the Crystal Castle. Ghislaine, with Gaston and Quentin playing knights nearby, gathered holly and berries, which she placed in the basket on the ground at her booted feet. Laudine, keeping a watchful eye on Quentin—the older, stronger boy—collected fragrant white hellebore blossoms near the stream at the edge of the forest.

Ghislaine's woodcutter husband Gaspard, having chopped an ample supply of firewood, hollered to the two boys, "I'm finished. Let's go practice with the knights."

With a whoop of joy, Gaston dashed across the courtyard to join his father, the lanky Quentin close behind, as the male trio disappeared toward the training field behind the castle.

Her heart full of holiday cheer, Viviane smiled brightly at her two companions, the three women bringing the Yuletide decorations into the welcoming *château*.

"This holly will make the conservatory and ballroom look especially festive," Viviane exclaimed merrily, as she and Ghislaine wrapped the dark green garlands around the columns which flanked the two sets of windowed doors. Behind the castle, the shimmery surface of *le Lac de Diane* glistened in the gray morning light. "Beginning on the winter solstice—when our sons and their guests arrive—the musicians will play each night, continuing all through the twelve days of Christmas until *la Fête des Rois*—Three Kings' Day. We'll have dining, drinking, and dancing…it will be a most splendid Yuletide season."

"Sophie is such a wonder in the kitchen," Laudine crooned as she arranged fragrant bouquets of the Christmas Rose—sweet-smelling white hellebore blossoms. "I cannot wait for the *Réveillon* feast on Christmas Eve. And Gaston loves her *bûche de Noël*!"

Viviane laughed gaily, her heart full of joy. The servants Odille and Florette joined in the decorating, and soon the clean, green scent of pine entwined with the sweet smell of holly and the floral fragrance of hellebore blossoms throughout the festive Crystal Castle.

Seated now in Viviane's cozy corner nook off the kitchen, the three friends shared a cup of *tisane* and gazed out the window at the gleaming lake.

"Esclados will be leaving in a few days, to bring two dozen horses to *le Château de Beaufort*," Laudine announced as she sipped her chamomile tea. "He's joining Lancelot the week before the Yuletide Joust, so they can finalize the preparations. More than a hundred visitors are expected, so they'll be erecting pavilions and overseeing the construction of a *berfrois* grandstand—for the royal audience and noble spectators." She smiled encouragingly at Viviane. "We three women can travel together in my carriage and arrive two days before the joust. My son Gaultier has prepared guest chambers for us all—a room for Esclados and me, another for Ghislaine, Gaspard, and Gaston. And a separate, private room for you, Viviane, on the same floor as ours." She grinned at Ghislaine, giving her hand an affectionate squeeze. "Although the men will be occupied with the horses and the contestants in the lists, we three can sit together in the grandstand and have a spectacular view of the joust."

"That's a lovely idea. We'll stay for the full three days—to watch the joust, enjoy the feast, and observe the royal wedding on the sixteenth. If we leave the following day, we'll be back here at the Crystal Castle well before the winter solstice. With plenty of time to enjoy our own Yuletide celebration." Viviane reached for the platter of almond cakes Sophie had left on the table, offering them to her guests.

Ghislaine accepted one, moaning with pleasure as she bit into the delectable confection. "Sophie is such a talented *pâtissière.* These are delicious." Wiping the corner of her mouth—upturned into a grin—she chuckled, "It's good that we're having one now, for once the boys see them, they'll be gone in an instant." Her expression became suddenly sorrowful, and she gazed forlornly at the lake. "Gaston will be so happy when he learns that Lancelot is taking him to Camelot…" A lone tear fell down her crumpled cheek. "But it breaks my heart to see him go."

Viviane slipped to Ghislaine's side, cradling her in a comforting embrace. "Lancelot comes home to Bretagne every summer. He'll bring Gaston here, to see you and Gaspard." She rocked Ghislaine in her arms, kissing the dark curls on her friend's head. "Just think how happy he'll be to meet his hero…and learn that he is to become a knight. His greatest wish will come true."

Ghislaine squeezed Viviane's reassuring arms. "You're right, of course." She raised her head, a grateful smile spreading across her face as Viviane sat down at her side. "For his Yuletide gift, Gaston will receive his own wooden sword. And a shield, with the three red bands of Lancelot's heraldry. He'll be so proud to bear his hero's coat of arms." Her bottom lip quivered, her sorrowful eyes brimming with tears anew as she held Viviane's comforting gaze. "I know you and Laudine both went through this with your own sons." She stared unseeingly into her cup, her quavering voice barely audible. "After longing for a child for so many years, to finally have him… and now…to have to let him go…" She buried her face in her hands, lowering her head onto the table.

Laudine silently rubbed her friend's shuddering back.

After a few moments, Ghislaine sat up, inhaled deeply, and wiped her tears away with a sad smile. "My Yuletide wish is to see him happy. That will fill my heart with unspeakable joy."

"Like you, Ghislaine. I want my sons to be happy." Laudine sipped her tisane as she gazed pensively at the lake. "Gaultier already is. He'll inherit our castle…and with so many lady friends, he'll have no trouble finding a wife when he's ready. Cardin is betrothed to the Lady Charlotte—she'll be coming here with him for the winter solstice, before they travel together to her family's estate for Christmas. He is very happy as well."

Compassion shone on Laudine's face as she spoke softly to Viviane. "But Bastien…personal royal guard to the princess… His prestigious duty will require him to serve faithfully at her side." Anguish blazed in her amber eyes. "While the woman he loves is married to another man. A man who will become *his king*."

Viviane quickly looked away, her own son Lancelot's similar suffering for Queen Guinevère an acute, unrelenting pain that gnawed at her heavy heart. With a shaking hand, she gulped her tea, struggling to regain her composure. Her legs quivered under the wooden table.

"My Yuletide wish," Laudine said longingly, as Viviane met her ethereal gaze, "is for Bastien to find the happiness he so richly deserves."

Viviane inhaled deeply and sighed. "Like you, my dear friends, my Yuletide wish is for my son to be happy. Although we all know he can never have the woman he loves… perhaps making Gaston's dreams come true will bring Christmas joy to Lancelot's loving, generous heart."

Ghislaine raised her cup of chamomile tea. "Let's toast. May the Yuletide Joust bring a fine husband to Princess Gabrielle and a worthy king to the throne of Finistère. May the holidays be merry and bright. And may all our Yuletide wishes come true."

With a joyous grin, Viviane added cheerfully, "May this be a most wondrous winter solstice in the glorious Crystal Castle."

Chapter 7

Hard as a Nail

Ugolin Cauchon was a scrawny, balding man with a prominent, beaklike nose and black, scornful eyes that glinted with unspeakable cruelty. Painfully thin, clumsy, and gangly, he'd been subjected to endless, sniggering torment as a child, relentlessly ridiculed for his physical weakness and hideously pockmarked face. Inept as a horseman, incapable with a sword, he was mercilessly humiliated for his frail frame and dominated into submission by forceful, formidable foes. Goaded and tortured with stinging shame, he'd been taunted with the nickname *Ugolin le Clou*—for he was skinny as a nail.

Unlike his older brother Roland—a ruggedly handsome, powerful knight—Ugolin had been a lonely, despised adolescent, filled with loathing and contempt, venting his fury and jealousy with cruelty and malice.

He'd begun by torturing small animals, reveling in their squeals of terror and anguish, thrilled with the power of inflicting pain and death. He'd progressed to tormenting children, severely beating and flogging servants, amputating fingers and toes for minor infractions. He'd whipped and slashed horses, maimed dogs, and strangled cats. And found indescribably delicious sexual satisfaction with weak, whimpering women.

His father, Robert Cauchon, *le Marquis de Nantes,* was a shipping merchant whose castle, l*e Château de Pornic*—ideally located at the mouth of the Loire River—granted him control of all trade along the coast of western France. Through his close association with the infamous pirate Balthazar, *le Marquis de Nantes* had amassed an enormous fortune and had introduced his despicable son to an endless entourage of merciless, mercenary knights, eager to inflict Ugolin's iron will.

So that the once disparaging, demeaning nickname evolved into an exultant epithet.

Ugolin le Clou.

Hard as a Nail.

Ugolin stood gazing out the enormous window of his father's solar, watching the turbulent ocean crash against the rocky cliff far below *le Château de Pornic*. Lightning flashed in the dark sky, the raging storm pelting sleet and freezing rain against the glass. At the sound of booted footsteps entering the informal conference room, Ugolin took his place at the end of the rectangular wooden table, opposite his father—the man unabashedly ashamed to have sired such a worthless, useless son.

Although his dark hair and trimmed beard were now streaked with gray, Robert Cauchon still held the rugged build of a seasoned warrior who had successfully defended his *marquisat* of Nantes and the *Château de Pornic* in many a battle. Shrewd, scornful eyes held his loathsome stare as servants filled pewter goblets while his brother Roland, the pirate Balthazar, and four mercenary knights entered the room to join Ugolin and the cold, calculating *châtelain*. "Greetings, everyone. Please be seated and enjoy the fine mead. I've requested this conference today to discuss the implications of the upcoming tournament at *le Château de Beaufort*."

Once the six men were settled around the table, imbibing mugs of mead, *le Marquis de Nantes* addressed his assembled guests.

"King Guillemin of Finistère has announced a Yuletide Joust, in which he will grant his daughter's hand in marriage to the champion." Derision and contempt in his sinister sneer, Robert Cauchon glared at Ugolin with thinly veiled disgust. "Since my younger son lacks skill with horse, lance, and joust—and since it is essential that he win the tournament—I have summoned you today to discuss how we shall make that happen."

The rich baritone voice of his older brother carried confidently across the table. "We'll appoint a champion to compete on his behalf." Roland gestured to the scarred, burly brute at his side. "Sir Tréguier is undefeated in the joust. He can win the princess—and the kingdom—for my brother. And, in recompense for his valorous achievement, Tréguier could be appointed as King Ugolin's champion. Paid handsomely in silver. And awarded an estate with a fine *manoir*."

Robert Cauchon nodded in judicious contemplation as he eyed the scarred, rugged knight.

"With several fine stable hands to assist with his own steed," Roland continued, expertly embellishing his proposition, "Tréguier could covertly arrange for other competitors' horses to fall ill. Or suffer an injury. Thereby ensuring his success. A guaranteed victory for Ugolin, regardless of the means."

Ugolin abruptly stood and strode briskly to the window, anger and resentment burning in his bitter gullet. His entire life, he'd never pleased his exigent, cynical father. Never compared to Roland's superior strength and skill. Never won anything on his own.

Until now.

He'd devised his own infallible plan.

He would indeed marry the Princess Gabrielle and obtain her father's throne. And once coronated, Ugolin would nullify *le Traîté Maritime*—the debilitating treaty prohibiting piracy on the Breton seas, ratified by a trio of Celtic kings: Tristan of Lyonesse, Marke of Cornwall, and Guillemin of Finistère.

With the treaty revoked, the pirate Balthazar would be free to seize ships and pillage ports, taking advantage of the myriad coves and inlets along the coast of Bretagne to conceal the confiscated bounty.

Enabling Ugolin to amass even more wealth than his invidious, invective father.

With King Tristan of Lyonesse in Ireland for his wife's coronation, King Marke of Cornwall recovering from a recent Viking attack, and King Guillemin of Finistère being slowly poisoned by the new *healer* whom Ugolin was paying well—the timing for his flawless gambit was perfect.

For the very first time in his wretched, worthless life, Ugolin Cauchon would triumph.

He'd subjugate his imperious father—the arrogant Marquis de Nantes.

And become more *puissant* than the pompous Philippe of Paris.

The powerful King of France.

To implement his stratagem, Ugolin had recently purchased the Tower of Kerloch, a fortress perched high on a peninsular cliff overlooking the sea. He'd spoken privately with Sir Tréguier and the three knights seated at his father's conference table, promising them a small fortune for their imperative role in his success. And Balthazar had generously provided a fleet vessel, prepared for the clandestine voyage south by sea.

The thrill of power surging up his scrawny spine, Ugolin spun to confront his father's insidious sneer.

What I lack in physical prowess, Father, I compensate with acuity and audacity.

"You are right that Sir Tréguier is our finest champion," Ugolin drawled, challenging Roland's inquisitive gaze. "But other competitors also excel at the joust. Thérouac of Dinan. Bergeron of Fougères. Audric of Sauterne. Any one of them might win Gabrielle's hand. Perhaps exchange horses unexpectedly at the last minute."

He strolled to the table, swallowed a great gulp of mead, and wiped his narrow mustache with long, skeletal fingers. "I cannot risk the possibility of losing."

Balthazar watched him intently, greed and malice glinting in his beady black eyes.

"Which is why I have devised an altogether different strategy. One that requires the prowess of the unparalleled knights seated at this prestigious table. And the assistance of my marauding friend." One side of his thin mouth curled up in a wicked grin as he held the pirate's rapt gaze.

Triumphant and exultant, Ugolin smirked at his skeptical, suspicious father. "We abduct the princess."

Roland and his fellow knights exchanged surprised glances as Ugolin unfolded his ingenious plan. "My spies have informed me that Princess Gabrielle practices weaponry each day with her personal royal guard, Sir

Bastien de Landuc. A dozen knights stand watch at the edge of the forest near an open field at the top of a cliff." He inclined his balding head to the scarred, burly Tréguier. "You and your men will take out the guards, abduct the princess, and bring her to me in Balthazar's awaiting ship. We'll sail south and keep her imprisoned in my newly acquired fortress—*La Tour de Kerloch*."

Ugolin glowered at the derisive, disparaging countenance riddled with contempt. Years of criticism, condemnation, and cynicism poisoned his embittered soul as he held his father's judgmental stare. "Although I cannot wield a soldier's sword, Father, I certainly can wield the one between my legs. I 've already sired a score of bastards on castle servants, tavern wenches, and meek maidens." He let out a lusty, lascivious laugh. "I'll simply keep Princess Gabrielle in my tower. Pump my potent seed into her until I get her with child. And, once she is pregnant, I'll force her father's hand."

He snickered with salacious delight. "An infinitely more pleasurable—and infallible—means of claiming the kingdom of Finistère." Ugolin drained his goblet and slammed it down on the table. "Ugolin le Clou. Hard as a fucking nail."

Chapter 8

The Fleeting Taste of Freedom

Embers glowed in the stone hearth along the wall of her royal bedroom, a salty spray cleansing the cool night air through the narrow opening of her window overlooking the sea. A symphony of stars twinkled in the dark, clear sky as Gabrielle arose from her bed and pulled a brown woolen frock down over her cotton chemise.

As Bastien had suggested, she'd feigned illness, allowing her attendants to undress and tuck her in bed with a cup of chamomile *tisane*. Alone at last, she stood in front of her mirror to plait her long, thick hair, tucking the braids high upon her head under a plain white wimple. Satisfied that she looked like a meek servant, Gabrielle quietly exited her royal chambers, lowering her head to avert the watchful eyes of the pair of guards stationed at her bedroom door, carrying the tray with the empty cup of tea down to the kitchen.

While other domestics scurried about with steaming platters of roast venison, fresh fish, and pitchers of ale to serve the castle occupants in the Great Hall, Gabrielle ducked into the pantry.

Where Bastien—clad like a huntsman in a heavy brown woolen cloak—awaited, his deep green eyes ablaze with mystery and promise. Her heart fluttering wildly, her mouth suddenly dry, Gabrielle placed a shaking hand against the wall to brace herself on weakened knees.

"This way, my lady." With chivalrous panache, Bastien opened the heavy wooden door and bowed, gallantly sweeping his arm for her to precede him down the stairs to the buttery.

Past the wooden barrels of ale and bottles of wine.

Out into the freedom of the starry, starry night.

****

The vibrant, lively atmosphere welcomed Gabrielle as Bastien led her into the noisy tavern where serving women with appetizing trays of aromatic food and tankards of ale circulated among boisterous, ebullient guests. Seating themselves at a tiny corner table, they ordered *le plat du jour*—trenchers of succulent roast boar dripping with honey—and hefty goblets of golden mead.

As she savored the salty pork and they sipped the sweet, honeyed wine, Gabrielle glanced around the jubilant hall, gaily decorated for the Yuletide season with garlands of shiny green holly and bright red berries draped along the wooden walls. Over the hearth where a blazing fire snapped and crackled, boughs of wintry evergreens decked the mantel, filling the festive air with the crisp, clean fragrance of pine. Musicians regaled the spirited crowd with vielles, rebecs, harps, and flutes, the lively melodies inviting patrons to swirl and twirl in a capricious *carole* upon the spacious floor.

"Would you like to dance?" Bastien wiped the mead from his grinning mouth with a corner of his linen napkin, a bemused gleam in his verdant gaze as he stood, extending an outstretched hand.

Breathless with anticipation, she accepted his offer,

her heart skipping a beat at the sizzling touch of his calloused fingers and the scorching flames of his emerald eyes.

Hand in hand, Bastien led Gabrielle to join the circle of dancers whose smallest fingers were linked together as they spun in a group around the perimeter of the floor. Individual couples took turns dancing in the center of the ring, each pair attempting to outperform the others while the exterior circle whooped and whirled.

A hearty grin stretching across his rugged, handsome face, Bastien pulled her into the midst of the cavorting crowd, spinning in circles as she shrieked with glee. Clutched tightly against his broad chest, chiseled arms wrapped snugly around her waist and back, Gabrielle melted into his supportive, enticing embrace. Burying her nose discreetly into the tuft of dark hair peeking out of his dark green tunic, she inhaled his heady scent of leather, horses, musk, and spice.

And swooned, overwhelmed with want.

Laughing and gasping for air, they staggered back to the table, sat down, and ordered more mead. Drunk with joy, Gabrielle smiled gratefully and exuberantly at Bastien. "Thank you for this memorable evening. For enabling me to experience freedom. It's a night I'll never forget…something I'll treasure forever."

His dazzling smile scorched her soul.

While the music and merriment continued in the background, Gabrielle gazed into the golden mead in her goblet. Her throat constricted into a tight lump. "I'm afraid of the future, Bastien. I don't want to be given away to a stranger."

An array of emotions blazed in his intense eyes.

Anger. Despair. Jealousy. Frustration.

"You 're a champion. The Master of Horse…" She frantically searched his anguished face, her voice breaking as she choked out the words. "Could you… compete in the joust?" Unwanted tears brimming, she quickly dashed them away and averted her eyes, tracing a finger around the rim of her goblet. "My Yuletide wish… is for *you* to be the champion." Mustering her last bit of courage, she raised her hesitant gaze to his. "And win my hand."

He grasped her clutched fist, opened it flat against his cheek, and tenderly kissed the inside of her palm. Wrapping her fingers within his own, he tucked her hand under his chin, as if it were a priceless treasure. "Nothing would bring me greater joy. But I cannot compete in the joust." He placed her hand reverently upon the table, reluctantly retracting his own. Embittered eyes bore into her heart. "I have no title of nobility. No lands or inheritance of my own. Nothing to offer a wife, let alone a princess. I am utterly unworthy of your royal hand."

The haunting melody of a mournful ballad soared from a troubadour's mellow harp, its plaintive notes and lyrics expressing the sorrow in Gabrielle's soul.

"How I long to know her love,
And yet so little learn
I cannot keep from wanting her
In passion though I burn
She stole my heart and all of me
Yet we are worlds apart
Without her, nothing's left for me
But the yearning in my heart."

A wave of desperation flooded as her pulse began to race. This was her last chance.

Lancelot and Sir Esclados would soon arrive with

the horses for the tournament. The entire castle would come alive with preparations for the Yuletide Joust. Great-aunt Béatrice and her vulturous vipers would voyage from Paris, visiting nobles would fill every guest room, and Gabrielle would not have a moment of respite.

Tonight was her final, fleeting taste of freedom.

And she wanted to savor every delectable drop.

She gulped the rest of her mead, swallowing her trepidation as her heart hammered wildly.

Bastien refilled their goblets from the pitcher on the table. Eyes as green as the verdant forest caressed her face, bolstering her courage.

Gabrielle locked her gaze with his. "You once said you would do anything for me."

Impassioned eyes held hers. "I did. And I would."

Lively fiddles began anew, raucous revelry reborn. "Dance with me again." She was desperate to feel his arms around her…inhale his intoxicating scent. Maybe, in his arms, she could muster the nerve.

An achingly beautiful smile lit up his handsome face, a glint of joy sparkling in his dark eyes. He took her hand and led her back onto the dance floor where laughing couples swirled and twirled. He pulled her close, and she laid her face against the broad chest where his heart thumped against her cheek. She drank her fill of his earthy scent, drawing it deep into her lungs.

His sculpted body molding against hers, he whirled her in his arms as if she were part of him. As if they belonged together. Two halves of a whole.

She lifted her face and kissed the hair at the base of his throat. His guttural moan reverberated into her body, making her breasts tingle. Keenly aware of the strong hand pressing against the small of her back, the hardness straining at her stomach, the muscular thighs entwined with her own, Gabrielle's knees weakened under her plain homespun gown.

I must ask him now. I'll never have the chance again.

"I want you to do something for me, Bastien." She buried her nose in his heaving chest.

"Anything, Gabrielle. Ask, and it is yours." A fierce longing blazed in his feral eyes.

Her legs trembling, she swallowed forcibly and met his intense gaze. "Before I am forced to submit to a husband against my will..." her voice was a barely audible whisper. "I want to give myself to the man I choose." Desperate tears filled her imploring eyes. "Please, Bastien... reserve us a room. And grant me this freedom before it is taken away."

****

He shook with a desire so strong he couldn't move.

Every fiber of his being yearned for her.

He'd loved her his whole wretched life. Suffered an inexorable, irresistible yearning—to the point of physical pain—longing to make her his. And now, she was offering him the impossible. The chance to bathe her in exquisite pleasure and the sublime joy of his love.

Before she was forced to suffer the brute.

The man who would become her husband and king.

Ugolin le Clou.

Jealous rage flared in his scorching veins. He wanted to kill the bastard. Keep Gabrielle for himself. He, Bastien—Master of Horse and expert jouster, trained by the legendary Sir *Lancelot du Lac*—would surely win the tournament. And yet, without a title of nobility, he was ineligible to compete for her hand.

Impotent fury sickened his soul.

A future together was impossible. But…they did have tonight. An evening to cherish forever. A fountain of memories to slake the thirst of an empty, endless existence without her.

Her desperate eyes searched his, breathlessly awaiting the response.

He brushed his lips gently across hers and whispered softly in her ear. "It will be my greatest honor. And most intense pleasure." Wrapping an arm around her shivering shoulders, he escorted her to their small table, seated her, and poured a goblet of mead. Firelight danced in her dark green gaze. "I'll be right back."

****

Gabrielle gulped down her mead, her legs quivering under the table, as she watched Bastien speak to the innkeeper behind the wooden bar. The portly, balding man wiped his hands on his apron, accepted coin from Bastien, and handed him a large metal key.

Primal desire blazing across his rugged face, Bastien returned to the table, grasped Gabrielle's trembling hand, and led her to the stairwell in the far corner of the inn.

Up to the second floor.

Down a quiet corridor.

And into the private room where she would savor the exquisite, ephemeral taste of fragile, fleeting freedom.

The door closed softly behind her. Inside the small room with wooden walls, Gabrielle lit a beeswax candle on the nightstand table beside the bed, the sweet smell inviting and welcoming. Her heart raced as Bastien locked the door, laid the key on top of the table, and turned to face her, a fierce hunger burning in his dark, feral eyes.

He removed his hooded cape, hung it on the metal hook beside the door, and unstrapped his sword, which he stood against the wall in the corner of the room. His scarred, brutally handsome face aflame, he approached Gabrielle and unfastened her cloak, the touch of his calloused fingers sending shivers down her spine. He strode across the room, hung her cape over his own, and returned to stand in front of her, watching as she removed the wimple and unbraided her long red hair. Dark eyes smoldering, he buried his hands in the thick, loosened locks, bringing strands to his aquiline nose, inhaling the essence as if it were the fragrance of a rare, exotic flower.

"How I love your glorious hair…" he murmured, adoring her tresses with reverent lips as he stepped softly toward her.

Gabrielle's stomach twitched as her breath hitched.

"I have longed to do this my entire life. I never dreamt this night would be possible… Let me show you how much I yearn for you." The rich timbre of Bastien's deep voice reverberated into her very bones, the low rumble strumming her like a mellow harp. Candlelit desire danced in his dark green eyes.

His lips worshipped her hand, a delicious warmth spreading throughout her body as he sucked each of her fingertips and thumb. A deep, hollow ache pulsed between her thighs.

He drew her close, wrapping sinewy arms around the small of her waist, moaning when she ran her fingers through his thick hair to stroke the back of his head. Lowering his bristled face to hers, he caressed her cheek, the masculine stubble intensely arousing, his breath a heated whisper in her ear. Pulling her firmly against him so she could feel his desire, his greedy lips sought her bare shoulder, then her neck, his insistent mouth and earthy, primal scent igniting a liquid fire in her loins. His smooth lips grazed hers, parting them gently with a tender tongue, deepening the kiss as he delved and probed, the hardness of his body making her throb with need.

Bastien eased the neckline of her dress and chemise down over her shoulders, baring her breasts with a guttural groan. He stroked the tender flesh, warm lips following his gentle fingers, licking and sucking until she swooned. Letting the garments puddle on the floor at her feet, he removed her boots and helped her step over the gowns as he led her toward him, his ardent gaze roving over her nude, quivering body. “By the Goddess, you are beautiful,” he whispered, calloused hands exploring her exposed skin, sending chills everywhere he touched. Ravenous, he crushed his lips against hers, his tongue prodding and penetrating, his eager mouth roving over her tender skin as he feasted on her flushed flesh.

He came up for air, his face feral and fierce. Emerald eyes ablaze, he locked her in his intense gaze as he removed his soft tunic and tossed it on the floor. Gabrielle’s knees buckled at the site of his chiseled arms overhead, the sculpted chest covered with dark hair, a trail leading down his taut, muscled abdomen to disappear into the woolen breeches where the hard outline of his body strained against the waistband.

The wet warmth between her thighs overwhelmed Gabrielle with want.

He approached her slowly, a ravenous hunger in his

savage eyes. He caressed her shoulders, running his warrior hands down her shivering arms, his thumbs stroking the tips of her breasts, making her nipples harden and ache.

Whimpering softly, she touched the dark hair on his chest, marveling at the rough texture against his smooth, rippled skin. The masculine scent of pine, leather, horses, and fresh sweat beckoned her. Beguiled her. Bewitched her.

Bastien's warm mouth sought her tingling breasts, his skilled tongue swirling, his lips sucking and swallowing until her legs could no longer support her weight. He gently laid her down on the bed and spread her legs to examine every inch of her with famished eyes.

"How I long to taste you," he whispered huskily, kneeling on the bed as he lowered his lips between her trembling thighs. "Delicious," he hummed, his tongue licking and probing the tender flesh, the vibrations of his deep voice a musical melody of physical pleasure. Rising onto his knees, he provocatively licked the first two fingers of his right hand. Impassioned eyes aflame, he held her gaze as his slick fingers penetrated her, eliciting moans of pleasure as she writhed under his adept touch. He returned his ardent, adoring mouth to her soft curls, his wicked tongue stroking the tender nub in rhythm with the steady pulsation of his strong, insistent hand.

Gabrielle's body tensed and tightened, the pressure mounting intolerably as Bastien increased the consistent rhythm of his caresses. When she could bear no more, a pleasure so intense it was nearly painful washed her in waves of impossible bliss as her body contracted on his fingers and quivered under his tongue.

He grinned, licking his lips and fingers, as he stood

and removed his breeches, his hardened body released at last from the confines of restrictive clothing. Gabrielle's breath caught at the seductive sight of his ardent arousal, a hollow ache swelling as she parted her legs and opened her arms to welcome him.

Positioning himself between her trembling thighs, he hovered over her, dark hair tumbling forward over his broad shoulders, fervent eyes ablaze with emerald fire. Sliding calloused, warrior hands under her full hips, he tilted her pelvis up, probed the entrance he sought. And plunged inside.

Pleasure surged as she wrapped her arms around his muscled back, her legs around his thrusting hips, pulling him deeper and deeper into her. She kissed his tightly flexed shoulder, savoring the salty taste, melding her body, her spirit, her essence with his. Matching his pounding pulses, the tension rising to an agonizing peak, her body clenched his in a tight grip, clamping on desperately until she convulsed under his shuddering bulk, contracting and extracting every last drop of his abundant seed.

"By the Goddess," he moaned contentedly a few moments later. "I have never known such intense pleasure." Raising a satisfied face to gaze down upon her, he lowered his lips to softly graze hers. "I love you, Gabrielle. I always have. And I always will." He kissed her again, the tender touch of his soft lips sending ripples of pleasure down her spine. His body slipped from hers, and he laid down beside her on the bed, cradling her in protective arms. "My sword. My heart. My life. I am yours."

She buried her nose in the dark hair on his chest, inhaling his scent deep into her lungs. "And I am yours.

I have loved you ever since I first saw you when I was ten years old." She raised herself onto one arm, playfully twirling his chest hair into peaks and rubbing them out again. His dark eyes danced in the candlelight. "Thank you for this precious gift. The freedom to give myself to the man I love. I will treasure this night always."

Brushing a lock of dark hair away from his bristled face, Gabrielle leaned down to kiss his full lips. Her heart clenched in a tight vise at the thought of a stranger—her future husband—bedding her in two short weeks. Eyes brimming, she lowered her gaze to focus on his alluring chest. How could she endure the advances of another man after giving herself freely to Bastien? Tears of anguish flowed down her cheeks. "I cannot bear the thought of anyone but you inside my body." She buried her face in the dark hair, crying softly onto his chest.

"Nor can I endure the idea of another man making love to you as I did just now. It tears out my heart and sickens my soul." He wrapped his arms around her, smothering her hair with kisses, groaning softly into her ear.

"I even imagined running away with you, assuming a new identity…" she whispered, raising forlorn eyes to meet his distraught, desperate gaze. "But I can't abandon my father… or my country. I'm a Viking warrior queen. And I will fight for Finistère." She kissed the thick hair on his torso, rising onto her knees to straddle him, her long hair falling in a cascade of flame around his broad shoulders. "But let's not waste a single moment tonight worrying about tomorrow." She sucked his lower lip into her own. "Let's savor the time that we have right now. So that the memories of this night together… will help us endure the agony of being apart." She rubbed the moist, tender flesh between her thighs against his hardening body. Plunged him again into her welcoming warmth. And rode her sublime stallion into sensuous, splendid surrender.

A while later, they reluctantly donned their discarded clothing.

Gabrielle plaited her hair, tucking the long braids up under the wimple.

Bastien strapped on his sword, fastened Gabrielle's cloak under her chin, and secured his own hooded cape. He blew out the candle, retrieved the key to lock the door, and escorted her back down the stairs to the raucous revelry of jubilant dancers and merry musicians. Returning the key to the innkeeper, he led her outside into the starry night, back to their tethered horses, and helped her climb into the saddle.

When they returned to the castle, he handed the horses' reins to a groom and guided Gabrielle back into the buttery among the caskets of ale. He stopped in front of a large barrel, pulled her into his arms, and crushed her lips with his. "Like you, I will always treasure tonight." He kissed her hand, stepped away, and walked over to a wooden casket of ale. Cupping his hand under the spout, he sloshed the liquid deliberately all over his clothing. With a sly grin, he chortled, "I'll reek of alcohol and act drunk. I'll create a disturbance—knocking things down as I cause a commotion. The guards will leave your door to investigate, laughing when they find me stumbling around. They'll guide me out to my quarters near the stables, and you'll be able to slip into your chambers unnoticed." He took her hand, leading her up the stairs and into the servants' area of the kitchen. "Wait here until I whistle. That will be your signal that it's safe to go upstairs to your room."

Intense eyes ablaze, he caressed her cheek and gently held her chin as his lips reached hers one last time. "Sleep well, my love. Until tomorrow morning, when we practice weaponry…for the last time."

In a flash, he was gone, leaving Gabrielle quivering in the dark, longing for his touch.

A few minutes later, she heard the scraping of furniture and the crash of a metal platter upon the floor. Booted footsteps hurtled down the stairs, and the low rumble of chuckling men assured her that Bastien's ruse had succeeded. At his whistle, she slithered from the dark kitchen, past the wrought iron sconces where candles flickered on the stone walls. Up the wooden stairs, down the empty corridor, and into her cold, silent room.

She removed the wimple and unbraided her locks, remembering the sensuous feel of his hands and the delicious way he kissed and inhaled the scent of her hair. Folding the peasant gown neatly, she placed it on her vanity table next to the wimple and strode over to the window to gaze out at the waning moon.

Stars winked in the night sky. An owl hooted to a mate. The crisp smell of winter wafted in the briny breeze.

With a sorrowful sigh, Gabrielle turned away from the bleak, black night.

Climbed into her lonely feather bed.

And dreamed of Bastien.

Chapter 9

Last Lesson

The cold, salty bite of the December wind stung her cheeks and whipped loose tendrils from her long braid as Gabrielle galloped wildly across the heathered moor. Her horse, Marivée, loved the exhilaration as much as her rider as they flew across the grassy plain toward the expansive plateau on the peninsular clifftop where she would have her last weaponry lesson today with Bastien, riding closely at her side.

In ten short days, the Yuletide Joust would begin.

The champion would become her husband.

Her lord.

Her king.

And Gabrielle's fleeting freedom would end.

She couldn't bear the idea of being handed over—like a piece of property—to the winner of the tournament. After giving herself freely to the man she loved, Gabrielle couldn't imagine anyone other than Bastien de Landuc in her marriage bed. And the thought of Ugolin le Clou becoming her husband made her positively ill.

A shiver of dread rippled up her spine.

When they arrived at the practice field, she and Bastien dismounted and tethered their horses at the edge of the forest where the royal guards remained on horseback to stand watch. Savage waves crashed against the craggy cliff far below the plateau, sending frothy, salty spray into the clouds where a flock of squawking white gannets flew overhead. Her heart as bleak as the gray sky, heavy with sorrow and loss, Gabrielle unsheathed her sword, bent her knees, and prepared for their last lesson together.

His emerald eyes aflame, Bastien beckoned her to attack. She lunged; he parried, bringing the tip of his sword around in a downward slice, causing her to step back. Just as she circled around to launch a new strike, the sudden clash of metal, angry shouts of men, and clamor of pounding hooves announced an ambush.

While the mounted guards battled invaders who appeared out of nowhere, six horsemen clad as peasants in hooded cloaks thundered out of the dense forest, headed directly toward them. Swords drawn, four descended upon Bastien while two others halted, dismounted, and swarmed Gabrielle.

Bastien had trained her well; she was skilled and adept with the blade. But while she clashed swords with one assailant from the front, the other slammed his shield against the backs of her knees, causing them to buckle as she collapsed to the ground. The first attacker disarmed her and quickly retrieved the fallen sword, while the second slid a powerful arm under her bent torso, lifting her kicking and screaming off the ground, restraining her in a strangling chokehold.

Her heart pounding out of her chest, she strained futilely against his unyielding grip, frantically scanning the embattled plateau for Bastien.

Swords colliding, shields crashing, grunts heaving, he was heavily engaged in battle, having killed three of his attackers, their mutilated bodies in a bloodied heap at his feet. Anguish blazing across his impassioned face, he dauntlessly fought the fourth, struggling desperately to reach Gabrielle.

One of her assailants—the huntsman who had retrieved her sword—strapped it to his horse's saddle and briskly led the animal toward Gabrielle's captor, a wicked gleam in his dark, cruel eyes.

I cannot let them take me. Think! Remember what Bastien taught you. Break free!

Balancing on her left foot, she rammed her right boot into his sensitive kneecap with all her might as she slammed the back of her hard skull into his vulnerable nose.

Howling in pain, he released her, one hand flying to staunch the profusion of gushing blood, the other seeking to assuage his damaged knee.

Gabrielle swiftly unsheathed the dagger from her waist, spun in a vicious circle, and slashed her assailant's throat. He dropped forward onto his knees, clutching his neck and sputtering blood as he gasped for air, falling onto his side as dark liquid pooled in a thick puddle under his heinous wound.

Stunned at the sight of a crazed woman warrior, the second assailant stood frozen in utter stupefaction as Gabrielle unerringly hurled her dagger into his villainous heart. He careened face first onto the cold, hard ground.

Bastien shouted to her, his final opponent slain on the battlefield behind him. "Gabrielle! To the cave!" He gestured to her assailant's horse as he leapt into the saddle of one of his own attackers.

With her booted foot, she quickly rolled the lifeless huntsman onto his back and retrieved her dagger, returning it to the strap at her waist. She ran to his horse, withdrew her sword, sheathing it as she climbed adroitly into the saddle. She cast a quick glance at Marivée, tethered at the far edge of the forest. There was no time to run across the plain. Goddess willing, if she survived, Gabrielle would return for her beautiful, beloved horse.

The distressed baritone of Sir Pontivy—the First Knight of *le Château de Beaufort*—bellowed across the battlefield. “Save the Princess! Go!”

With Bastien close behind, Gabrielle galloped away from the bloody *mêlée* where her beleaguered, outnumbered, fiercely loyal royal guards defended her to the death.

She tore through the forest, weaving through the familiar trees, arriving at last to the wooded ledge with the path leading down to the sheltered shore. They flew out of the saddles and released the horses, slapping their rumps to drive them off into the forest, leading pursuers in the wrong direction, away from the beach.

Bastien grabbed her hand and dashed down the narrow, steep path to the sandy shore two hundred feet below the wooded ledge.

Adrenaline surging, her heart hammering, her mouth bone dry, Gabrielle ran across the beach with Bastien, through the hidden sea cave entrance, into the dark, secret tunnel. When they came to the trap door in the cave ceiling which led up into the castle, Bastien pushed it open, boosted her overhead, then pulled himself into the storage cellar within the foundation of *le Château de Beaufort.*

“I always unlock the door each time we train, in the event we ever want to get up into the castle. Never have we needed it more than today.” Taking her hand, he raced up the stone steps into the kitchen pantry, locking the door behind him as he shouted for his brothers. "Gaultier! Cardin! Summon the guards! We're under attack!"

Flustered servants flocking at his heels, he quickly brought Gabrielle into the royal solar where King Guillemin sat on his informal throne, looking out the large window at the savage sea crashing against the craggy cliff far below the castle. At their sudden approach, the king turned abruptly toward them, astonishment written across his gaunt, weary face.

Bastien seated a breathless Gabrielle next to her father and beckoned the chamberlain Ezhvin. "The princess is distraught, for there was an attempt to abduct her during our training today. See to her needs. I must return at once to aid Sir Pontivy."

He kissed her hand, his intense eyes aflame. "Tell your father what happened. I'll return as soon as possible." In a flash, he was gone, leaving Gabrielle shaking from the assault.

And terrified that Bastien might not return.

"What happened, Gabrielle? You were attacked?" Concern, shock, and outrage warred in her father's assessing gaze as a capable attendant placed a steaming mug of *tisane* on the table in front of her with a polite curtsey and discreetly disappeared.

"Yes…while we were training," she gasped, swallowing a large gulp of the calming chamomile tea. She inhaled deeply, the sweet, herbal fragrance soothing her ragged nerves. "Dozens of armed horsemen stormed the forest and attacked my guards. Six descended upon us, swords drawn, and Bastien defended me. He saved my life, Papa. Not only did he slay four of the attackers, but the skills he taught me in self-defense enabled me to fight off my abductors and escape." Tears streamed down her flushed cheeks as she faced the anxious, overwrought king. "I killed them both, Papa. I… I… killed two men." She buried her face and sobbed into her hands, overwhelmed as the stark realization of what she had done finally hit her.

His gnarled hand softly stroked her disheveled hair. "Shh…" he whispered as he gently pulled a few stray strands from the side of her face, tucking them back into her unkempt braid. "You did what had to be done. Like a true Viking warrior queen, you fought with fury and slew your enemies."

Gabrielle raised her tear-streaked face to meet his proud, loving gaze.

"I am profoundly grateful to Sir Bastien de Landuc. Not only did he teach you weaponry and self-defense, but he valiantly defended you as your personal guard. I am forever indebted to him for saving your life." He kissed her trembling hand, his shining eyes brimming with gratitude. "I shall reward him handsomely—as befits this unparalleled act of valor."

Gabrielle's breath hitched and her stomach lurched.

"I shall grant Sir Bastien de Landuc a fiefdom—*un fief de dignité*. And a title of nobility—*la noblesse chevaleresque*—in honor of his chivalrous deed." Her father beamed as he affectionately pushed wayward wisps away from her face. "I shall ennoble him as *le Marquis de Cornouaille*, bestowing upon him not only the noble title, but the fiefdom of *la Cornouaille*—comprising the entire southern half of my kingdom of Finistère—with its magnificent castle, *le Château de Concarneau."*

The king smiled knowingly, leaning forward to wipe away her tears and tenderly caress her damp cheek. "With a title of nobility, Bastien will be eligible to compete in the joust. Goddess willing, he'll prevail—and win your hand. Thereby granting my Yuletide wish to see you properly wed before I die." He raised her shaking hand to his parched lips and bestowed a gentle kiss.

"Nothing would bring me greater joy, Papa." She lifted her eyes to meet his. "For I love Bastien de Landuc. I always have, ever since I first saw him." Gabrielle smiled softly at her generous father whose haggard face shone with paternal love. "Bastien taught me to ride, to care for Marivée..." She reverently traced her father's bony fingers with a loving thumb. "I am now expertly skilled with the sword, the dagger, the bow and arrow...all because of him." She lowered her lips to kiss her father's knotted knuckles. "Your Yuletide wish is to see me safely wed. And mine...is to be the winter solstice bride of Bastien de Landuc, *le Marquis de Cornouaille*." She cast the benevolent king a hopeful smile as she lovingly squeezed his brittle hand. "May both our Yuletide wishes come true."

The royal physician Isnard slithered into the room with a pewter goblet and bowed before the king. "Forgive the intrusion, Your Majesty, but it is time for your medicine."

Gabrielle observed the peculiar healer whose sparse, thin hair barely covered his balding pate. His hunched posture and lowered head gave the outward appearance of humility and subservience, yet his predatory gaze sent a shiver of dread up Gabrielle's spine as the enigmatic Isnard placed the chalice before the king.

"I'll drink it later. Set it down here for now." The

king indicated an area on the table before him.

"It is essential that you take it at the same time each day, Sire. As your royal physician, I must insist." Isnard bowed his head in reverent *obéisance*, but his dark eyes glinting with malice made the hairs on the back of Gabrielle's neck rise in warning.

"It always makes me groggy, and I wish to remain alert until my knights return with their report. Set the goblet here. You are dismissed, Isnard." King Guillemin's adamant tone brooked no refusal.

"As you wish, Sire. I shall return later to ensure that you have taken the proper dose. I'll also assess your condition and determine if any further treatment—such as a purging or bloodletting—is warranted. Until then, I bid you and the Princess Gabrielle good day." Isnard bowed reverently and exited the royal solar, suspicion and mistrust etched upon his sullen, sunken face.

Once the healer had left the room, Gabrielle whispered, "Papa… I am leery of your royal physician. He emits a malevolent aura." She sipped her chamomile tea, keenly observing her father over the rim of the cup. The king's complexion was pallid and gaunt; dark circles rimmed his eyes dulled with pain. "You have suffered from gout for several years but have just recently been plagued with stomach ailments. Isn't that right, Papa?"

The king summoned Ezhvin, waiting patiently against the wall beside a serving table. "Bring me a goblet of wine. And send for more chamomile tea for the princess."

"*Oui, Votre Majesté*." The royal chamberlain bowed humbly and discreetly disappeared to obey.

Gabrielle's father nodded in response to her question. "Yes, I've had horrible bouts of stomach pain, nausea, and vomiting. My disorders are getting worse, and my health is rapidly declining. That is why I called you home from Paris."

Ezhvin returned with a decanter of wine and a silver goblet. He filled the chalice, placed it before the king, and gestured for a female attendant to a serve a fresh cup of *tisane* to Gabrielle.

King Guillemin waited until his royal chamberlain and the kitchen servant departed before placing his hand over hers with a gentle squeeze. His voice quavered with emotion and his kind eyes glimmered in the afternoon light. "I do not expect to live much longer, *ma fille.* That is why it is essential that I see you wed as soon as possible." A sudden grimace of pain distorted his face as his hand sought his stomach. He hissed between clenched teeth.

Gabrielle glanced at the pewter goblet of medicine sitting on the table. "Papa, when did your stomach problems begin? This past summer?"

The king stretched sideways, as if to relieve his discomfort, picking up the silver chalice of wine Ezhvin had just poured. He swallowed a hearty gulp, wiped his mouth with the back of his hand, and reflected for a few moments before responding. "Yes, as a matter of fact. Around midsummer."

Gabrielle reached across the table for the goblet of herbal medicine and sniffed the questionable brew. A tangy, citrusy aroma that tingled her nostrils mingled with a repulsive musky, peppery odor that made her choke. She hastily set it down on the opposite side of the table, far away from her father. A ripple of unease crept up her spine.

"Papa…when did the healer Isnard become your

royal physician? Wasn't it just a few months ago?" Her limbs began to shake.

"Indeed, it was. He arrived here, with highest recommendations, to treat my recurring gout." King Gullemin looked down at his badly swollen ankle propped upon a low footstool at his side. A large red blister filled with an ominous yellow liquid had made wearing a boot painfully impossible. He winced as he repositioned the grotesquely distended foot. "Unfortunately, despite numerous treatments with leeches and maggots, foul-smelling ointments, and putrid elixirs—there has been no improvement."

Gabrielle reflected how Isnard had come to the castle this past summer. The same time her father's sudden stomach illness had begun. "And your digestive problems arose just as your royal healer began treating your gout." She leaned forward in her chair and clutched her father's hand as his uncomprehending gaze met hers. "Perhaps it is a coincidence, Papa…but I believe that Isnard is giving you herbs that harm rather than heal." She nodded to the suspicious goblet. "That medicine has a noxious, repugnant odor. I suspect it contains toxic herbs." She pulled the king's hand protectively to her chest. "Papa…promise me that you will not take any medicine that Isnard serves you. And that you will refuse any and all treatments that he recommends."

Gabrielle searched her father's baffled, bewildered face. "Bastien's mother, the Lady Laudine, is a Priestess of Dana. A respected healer who is very familiar with medicinal herbs. And Sir Lancelot's mother, the Lady Viviane, is the High Priestess of Avalon—a prestigious center renowned for healing. They will be arriving very soon for the Yuletide Joust." She nodded toward the pewter goblet with the loathsome brew. "I will place that elixir in a container and keep it for them to examine. Perhaps Laudine or Viviane can identify the contents and determine if it is indeed harmful, as I suspect." She scrutinized her father's weary face. "I will have them examine you as well, Papa." She brushed a strand of graying, greasy hair from his haggard face. "They might offer an alternative treatment and recommend a different healer. One who can restore your health."

The king smiled weakly and patted her hand, his face contorting in pain. In his stark, bleak gaze, Gabrielle saw futility, surrender, and despair. Her father had no hope of ever being cured. He had already accepted—perhaps even welcomed—his imminent death.

Smothering grief weighed upon Gabrielle's heavy heart.

She inhaled deeply and rose to her feet, smoothing her rumpled gown and tucking the wayward strands of hair back into her bedraggled braid. Reaching for the goblet, she announced to her father, "I'll store this potion in a stoppered vial and save it until Laudine and Viviane arrive in a few days."

A crisp, salty breeze wafted in through the narrow opening of the window where the thunderous surf crashed against the craggy cliff. Gabrielle glanced out at the turbulent ocean, the image of the hidden sea cave and secret tunnel flashing in her mind. Silently, she prayed that Bastien would safely return soon. Mustering a reassuring smile that belied her disquieted soul, she said brightly to her father, "Stay here and sip your wine. I'll be right back."

Clutching the goblet of herbal brew, she slipped from the royal solar with the intention of heading to the kitchen—when she spotted the healer Isnard lingering just outside the entrance door. An alarming wave of apprehension washed over her, and Gabrielle instantly decided not to leave her father unattended. Instead, she summoned the royal chamberlain, who waited patiently in the hallway. "Ezhvin, please come here. The king requests your assistance."

The humble, fiercely loyal Ezhvin had served King Guillemin for Gabrielle's entire life. She trusted her father's personal valet implicitly. When he dutifully approached the king, Gabrielle said quietly, "Please bring me a stoppered vial. I wish to store the contents of this medicine so that it may be analyzed. I suspect it might contain harmful herbs."

Ezhvin's large brown eyes widened in shock. He cast a worried glance at the ailing monarch slumped on the informal throne, his stomach clutched in obvious agony.

Gabrielle spoke softly into the chamberlain's ear. "Say nothing, but do not allow my father to consume any food or drink that you have not personally prepared —or supervised being prepared—from start to finish. I have no proof yet, but I suspect the healer Isnard is causing the king more harm than good."

The dependable valet nodded fervently, his solicitous, intelligent eyes steadfastly holding her gaze. "*Oui, Votre Majesté*. You have my word."

"Thank you, Ezhvin. My father and I are both extremely grateful for your impeccable, reliable service. I have the utmost confidence in your loyalty."

"I am honored and humbled by your kind praise, Your Highness." The royal chamberlain bowed deferentially to the king, then to Gabrielle, and departed to retrieve the stoppered vial.

Gabrielle returned to her father's side.

He adjusted himself in the velvet tufted chair, repositioning his swollen foot as he shifted to alleviate the pain in his abdomen. In response to his questioning gaze, she smiled comfortingly and replied, "I've decided to stay here with you." She kissed his cheek. "Ezhvin is fetching a vial for this elixir." She set the goblet of medicine down upon the table and refilled her father's wine chalice from the silver decanter, trying to dispel the anxiety which gripped her heart. Handing him the wine, she whispered fervently, "I pray that Bastien and the knights return soon. *Triumphant*."

Distraught about her father's frail health, suspicious of his nefarious healer, fearful for Bastien's safety and the welfare of the other knights, Gabrielle's stomach was clenched in a tight knot. She reached across the table to retrieve the suspicious herbal brew, gazing into its murky depths and waiting impatiently for Ezhvin's return.

A few moments later, he arrived with a glass flask, which Gabrielle filled with the herbed medicinal brew. She inserted the cork stopper into the neck of the small bottle and rose to her unsteady feet. "Ezhvin, stay here with the king." Gabrielle bent to kiss her father's withered cheek. "I'll be right back, Papa."

The stoppered flask clasped tightly in her fist, Gabrielle slipped from the solar and searched the corridor. The healer Isnard was nowhere in sight, so she hurried up the stone stairs, down the empty hall, and into her royal chambers. She closed and locked the door, her limbs aquiver, all jittery and jumpy. Striding across the room, she opened the carved wooden door of her massive oak armoire and retrieved a pair of white lace gloves from the top shelf. Placing the stoppered vial inside one of the gloves, she wrapped it within a ruffled petticoat, folded it carefully, and tucked the parcel behind her other garments at the back of the top shelf, concealing it from view.

Exhaling forcefully to calm her ragged nerves, she closed and locked the double doors of her armoire with the metal key, tucking it safely into the velvet pouch strapped to her waist.

I hope Bastien's mother and the Lady Viviane can identify the herbs in that disgusting brew. I truly believe it is toxic. But why would Isnard want to poison the king?

Gabrielle's knees buckled as the realization hit her.

For Ugolin le Clou.

He must be paying Isnard to poison her father! Slowly at first, to cause symptoms of illness. Continuously, so it would appear that the king suffered from a long-term affliction. And, once Ugolin won her hand in the Yuletide Joust, Isnard would undoubtedly administer a fatal dose. Everyone would believe her father had finally succumbed to his debilitating disease. Ugolin would be crowned King of Finistère.

And no one would suspect him of poisoning the king.

The bloody bastard!

Gabrielle vowed to prevent that from happening. Somehow, she would find a way to stop Ugolin le Clou.

And the poisonous *healer* Isnard.

By the Goddess, she hoped Bastien would return soon, reporting that the knights of Beaufort had successfully repelled the attack. She'd tell him about her suspicions. And Father would then tell him the wonderful news about the title of nobility, enabling

Bastien to compete in the joust. He was an expert horseman—trained by the legendary *Lancelot du Lac*, the greatest jousting champion in the entire Celtic realm. Bastien simply had to win the tournament—and her hand in marriage. She couldn't even consider any other possible outcome.

With Bastien as her husband, the threat of Ugolin le Clou would be squelched. And, with Bastien's mother Laudine and the Lady Viviane—two exceptionally gifted healers—properly treating her ailing father, perhaps he would return to good health and live many more years.

Her heart fluttering wildly at the thought of marrying the man she loved and the chance that her father could indeed recover, Gabrielle whispered a prayer with all the yearning in her hopeful heart.

Please, dear Goddess, help me save my beloved father. And please grant my Yuletide wish. That Bastien de Landuc will win my hand in the Yuletide Joust. And I shall be a winter solstice bride, wedded to the man I love.

Still anxious, yet tentatively optimistic, Gabrielle returned to the royal solar, pleased to see her father's color slightly improved by the wine and fresh ocean breeze.

He smiled as she kissed his crinkled, bristled cheek and sat down at his side.

Ezhvin refilled the king's goblet and poured one for her, which she accepted gratefully, the earthy, fruity flavor as delightful on her tongue as the relaxing warmth spreading through her tense body.

A commotion arose as Bastien, his brothers Gaultier and Cardin, and several harried knights brusquely entered the quiet solar.

At the sight of his scarred, bloody, handsome face, relief flooded Gabrielle's veins. *Thank the Goddess, he's alive!*

The knights removed their helmets and bowed before the king. Bastien spoke in a breathless voice. "Your Majesty, of the two dozen who attacked the royal guards, all but four have been slain. Three managed to escape before we arrived to reinforce Pontivy and his men, but one—although badly wounded—still lives."

"We'll make him talk." Gaultier's dark eyes blazed with hatred as he glanced at his younger brother Bastien. "He'll tell us who sent them."

King Guillemin sighed audibly. "I know who sent them." He raised his dejected, dispirited gaze to Bastien. "Ugolin le Clou." The king took a large gulp of wine and set his goblet down. "But I cannot make accusations without proof." He turned to Gaultier. "Did the attackers bear any coat of arms on shields or surcoats?"

"No, my king. They were dressed as ordinary huntsmen in plain woolen cloaks and breeches. But they wielded swords like highly skilled knights." Gaultier's fierce, dark eyes and sleek, black hair gleamed in the afternoon setting sun.

"Where is Pontivy?" The king searched the group of soldiers for the captain of his royal guards.

"He was killed in battle, Sire. Along with nine of our best knights. Only Yvain and Bruno survived the attack." Gaultier gestured to the two bloodied, battered knights who stood proudly before their king.

King Guillemin lowered his head, aggrieved by the loss of his champion. "An irreparable loss for the kingdom of Finistère. He was an incomparable swordsman and unparalleled knight." Eyebrows furrowed, he raised his regal gaze to Bastien's older brother. "Gaultier, you will replace Pontivy as my new champion. I hereby appoint you Captain of my Royal Guards, And First Knight of Beaufort. "

Gaultier knelt beside the king and kissed his royal ring. "It shall be my greatest honor, Sire."

As Gaultier returned to his place among the royal guards, King Guillemin addressed Yvain and Bruno, the two survivors of Pontivy's slaughtered men. "You both valiantly defended *le Château de Beaufort*. Each of you will be handsomely rewarded with a hefty bag of silver." Gabrielle's father turned from the grinning guards to behold Bastien, a generous glint in his regal gaze. "Bastien de Landuc, please approach. I wish to reward you as well."

Gabrielle held her breath as Bastien knelt at the king's feet, her gaze darting from her regal father to the man who held her heart. The champion who, Goddess willing, would prevail in the Yuletide Joust.

Become her wedded husband.

And the future King of Finistère.

King Guillemin's voice quavered with emotion. "I am deeply indebted and eternally grateful to you for saving my daughter's life today. In recompense for your intrepid valor, Sir Bastien de Landuc, I shall grant you *la noblesse chevaleresque*—a title of nobility for your chivalrous deed. I hereby bestow upon you the title of *le Marquis de Cornouaille* as I bequeath *un fief de dignité*—the fiefdom of Cornouaille, encompassing the southern half of my kingdom of Finistère, along with the magnificent *Château de Concarneau*."

Bastien raised an incredulous face, astonishment shining in his deep green eyes.

"As a titled member of nobility, you will be eligible to compete in the Yuletide Joust." King Guillemin grinned expansively at Gabrielle. "It is the Yuletide wish of my beautiful daughter—and my own as well—that you should prevail and win her hand. Rise now, with the royal blessing of your most grateful king."

Bastien stood proudly before the king, fierce eyes glued on Gabrielle.

King Guillemin summoned Ezhvin. "Send for a scribe and order a royal messenger to prepare for departure within the hour." He informed Bastien, "I shall write the official proclamation of nobility in the form of *lettres patentes* and send the document to Paris. In about a week, we'll receive the official decree from *le Parlement de Paris.* Just in time for you to compete in the Yuletide Joust."

Bastien stood in stunned silence as the king spoke to Gaultier, the new First Knight of Beaufort and Captain of the Royal Guards. "Have your men gather and prepare our fallen soldiers for an honorable burial and memorial tribute tomorrow. Burn the corpses of the enemy. And prepare for the arrival of Bastien's father, Sir Esclados le Ros, who is expected to arrive in two days with magnificent horses for the Yuletide Joust. Sir Lancelot will be arriving shortly thereafter with another two dozen mounts from his incomparable stables."

Gaultier bowed before the king. "*À vos ordres, Votre Majesté.*" With a jut of his chin, the new First Knight of Beaufort led his men from the royal solar to obey the king's command.

Ezhvin returned with the scribe, whose quilled pen meticulously drafted King Guillemin's official decree of nobility—*la noblesse chevaleresque*—for Bastien de

Landuc, the newly appointed *Marquis de Cornouaille.*

King Guillemin removed his signet ring, sealed the regal decree with wax, and tied the royal proclamation with red satin ribbon. He handed the *lettres patentes* to the ready rider, who was eagerly waiting at the scribe's side. "Ride hard, and change horses frequently, so that you arrive at *le Parlement de Paris* within two days. Come back immediately with the official sealed document. You will be well compensated upon your return. Depart at once."

"At your command, *Votre Majesté*. I shall return within five days."

As the royal messenger and scribe departed, the king grinned at Bastien. "Tonight, we celebrate your appointment as *le Marquis de Cornouaille."* To Gabrielle, he quipped, "I am sure you and *Monsieur le Marquis* have much to discuss. But you must excuse your king. For I need to rest and recuperate before tonight's impromptu feast."

With a weary smile, her father summoned Ezhvin, who, along with Bastien, helped the king rise to a stand. Another valet approached to replace Bastien, and the two royal attendants led the exhausted monarch from the solar to his royal chambers for a much-needed rest.

Alone at last with Bastien, Gabrielle flung her arms around his neck and covered his face with furious, frantic kisses. "Now you can compete in the joust and win my hand! Bastien, it is my Yuletide wish come true!"

He responded with a glorious smile that took her breath away as he crushed her in his powerful arms.

Hungrily devoured her eager lips.

And, in a ragged, husky voice, whispered in her ear, "Mine, too."

Chapter 10

A Flawless Gambit

La Tour de Kerloch was a formidable fortress perched on a jagged, treacherous cliff overlooking the tumultuous, turbulent sea. Inside its massive stone crenelated walls, Ugolin le Clou sat with his father, Robert Cauchon, and Onfroi—the wealthy and powerful *Vicomte de Vannes*—at a large rectangular wooden table in the well-appointed antechamber.

Ugolin stared in disbelief and disgust at the trio of incompetent, idiotic knights who stood at attention, having just returned to the castle.

Without the captive princess.

"*Where is she*?" he snarled at the burly, brawny Sir Tréguier. The intrepid knight who never failed.

"She escaped, my lord. Four of our men swarmed her royal guard, Bastien de Landuc—but he slew them all. Two others attempted to capture the princess, but she fought them off. And killed them both." Tréguier lowered his eyes in shame, averting Ugolin's icy glare.

Ugolin bolted to his feet, his chair toppling to the floor behind him. "*The princess* killed two highly trained, armed knights?" Incredulous, his mouth agape, he stared in stunned stupefaction at his disgraced, dejected, demoralized soldiers.

"With a dagger, my lord. She slit Enguerrand's

throat. And hurled the blade right into Vauquelin's heart. She and her guard escaped on horseback into the woods." Piers—second in command to Tréguier—examined the felted hat he held in his quavering hands.

"*And you did not pursue them*?" Livid with rage, spittle flew from Ugolin's scathing tongue.

"We did, my lord. We found the horses. Without their riders." Guarin, the third knight to have returned from the failed abduction of the princess, lowered his blond head in dishonor and disgrace.

"I send two dozen of my best men, and you three return in humiliating defeat. Twenty-one men were lost?" Ugolin stomped back and forth, pacing furiously in front of the window where the crashing waves of the thunderous surf depicted the pounding rage in his thundering heart.

His father's scornful sneer followed his every move.

"Giles was wounded, my lord. The knights of Beaufort… took him back to their castle." Tréguier's dark eyes reflected the dire implications of that capture.

Under torture, Giles would talk.

And inform King Guillemin of Finistère that Ugolin le Clou had sent the henchmen to abduct his royal daughter.

Sufficient grounds for retaliation.

Even outright war.

"Sit." Ugolin ordered the trio of disgraced knights to join his scowling father and scheming colleague as he took his own seat at the head of the table. He motioned to a servant, who promptly poured mugs of mead for all and discreetly retreated to his position next to the elegant sideboard against the rear wall. Ugolin drained the contents of his mug and slammed it down on the table.

The contrite failures flinched, nearly jumping out of their respective chairs.

Ugolin glowered at his father. "Isnard must eliminate Giles."

Robert Cauchon replied cautiously, "Indeed… before Giles can talk." The Marquis de Nantes drank from his goblet, eyeing his son over the engraved pewter rim.

"We need to ensure that Tréguier wins the Yuletide Joust. By any means." Ugolin raised his goblet for the servant to refill before continuing. He stared at the dark-haired champion who would represent him in the joust. "With your unparalleled skill, Tréguier, you will advance to the final match of the competition. To ascertain your triumph as the champion…" he drawled, handing a small burlap bag to the dark-haired knight, "…your squire will add this to the feed of your opponent's horse the morning of the joust."

Tréguier guardedly examined the contents of the sack.

"Yew needles. Extremely toxic. Mix them into the horse's hay." Ugolin gulped from his goblet and wiped his sullen mouth with the back of his hand. "When the tournament begins, the animal will become disoriented, uncoordinated, and jumpy. Enabling you to quickly unseat your rival. Kill his horse with your lance—thereby eliminating any suspicion of poisoning. You'll be declared the champion. Redeem yourself for today's calamitous defeat. And win me the coveted hand in marriage of the Princess of Finistère."

A valet appeared in the doorway. "My lord, the healer Isnard has arrived with an urgent message."

Ugolin shot a quick glance at his scowling father

before responding. "Bring him in."

His slight shoulders slumped, balding head lowered in humility, the healer Isnard slithered into the room. "Forgive the intrusion, Lord Ugolin, but I bear news of utmost importance."

"A chalice of mead for my honored guest." Ugolin snapped at an alert attendant who quickly complied. "Please, be seated, Isnard. I am anxious to hear your report."

With long, skeletal fingers, the macabre healer accepted the proffered beverage and swallowed a large gulp before speaking. Sinister delight danced in his dark eyes. "I was regretfully forced to flee *le Château de Beaufort* today, for the Princess Gabrielle suspects me of harming the king with my *herbal treatments.*" He grinned wickedly at Ugolin. "I overheard her tell her father that she plans to have the Lady Laudine—Sir Bastien de Landuc's mother—and the Lady Viviane, the High Priestess of Avalon, analyze the contents of the elixir which I attempted to serve the recalcitrant king this morning." He gulped more mead and set down his goblet. "Both ladies are skilled healers and would easily recognize the toxic herbs. Hence my decision to depart before being apprehended for attempted regicide." A feral grin bared his long, yellowed teeth. "But Lord Ugolin—I bear much more important news. Information that you will deem invaluable."

Ugolin leaned forward in eager anticipation. "You have certainly piqued my curiosity, Isnard. Impart this urgent message."

Beady black eyes scrutinizing the guests seated at the majestic oak table, Isnard hissed, "With a royal decree of *noblesse chevalresque,* King Guillemin has ennobled Sir Bastien de Landuc. Bestowing upon him the title of Marquis and bequeathing the fiefdom of *la Cornouaille* and *le Château de Concarneau.* As we speak, his royal messenger is en route to Paris with the official proclamation to be authenticated by *le Parlement de Paris* and King Philippe in *le Palais-Royal*."

Seething with frustrated fury, Ugolin shot to his feet. "As *le Marquis de Cornouaille*, Bastien de Landuc will be eligible to compete in the Yuletide Joust." He strode to the oceanfront window, the crashing waves evoking the rage in his bitter soul. "De Landuc is the Master of Horse at Beaufort. Trained by the legendary *Lancelot du Lac.*" He spun to glare at Tréguier. "He will be your competitor in the final round." Shaking with furor, Ugolin slapped his palms flat on the table and leaned menacingly into Tréguier's scarred, wary face. "Poison his horse. Charge with a sharpened lance. Kill the bloody bastard." He pushed away in indignant ire, rolled his head across his shoulders, and grabbed his goblet, sloshing the liquid over his quavering hand. Draining the contents in one long pull, he slammed the empty chalice down on the tablet, his anger echoing across the silent room.

"You say the messenger is en route to Paris as we speak?" The velvety voice of Onfroi, the *Vicomte de Vannes,* broke the unsettling stillness.

Isnard responded to the elegantly attired, shrewd nobleman seated beside Ugolin's pensive father. "Yes, as I was preparing to exit the castle this morning—ostensibly to fetch more herbs for the king's ongoing treatment—I saw the messenger ride away in great haste. I overheard him say he expected to arrive in Paris within two days."

Lord Onfroi remarked coyly, "I had planned to depart for Paris tomorrow. My wife Clothilde and her extravagant coterie of fine ladies expect me to escort them to *le Château de Beaufort* as noble spectators for the Yuletide Joust." His narrowed eyes glinted with cunning and malice. "However, in light of Lord Isnard's startling revelation, I shall instead leave at once, sending my men ahead to intercept King Guillemin's decree of nobility for Sir Bastien de Landuc." A predatory grin stretched slowly across the *vicomte's* serpentine face. "My riders will divert the delivery of that missive to *la Tour Kerloch,* rather than *le Parlement de Paris* on the *Île de la Cité.*" Onfroi smiled snidely, the delicate lace of the jabot at his neck a sharp contrast to the ruthless sneer on his hardened, wizened face. "If, against all odds. Sir Bastien de Landuc should miraculously prevail in the Yuletide Joust, you will simply demand that King Guillemin produce the official decree of the champion's title of nobility. Which, of course, he shall be unable to do. Since you, Ugolin le Clou, shall possess that precious document."

Malicious delight glowed in his veins. Ugolin grinned greedily, motioning for the obedient servant to refill the goblets of mead. When the task was complete, he raised his pewter chalice in tribute, proposing a triumphant toast. "To Lord Onfroi, *le Vicomte de Vannes*. For his magnificent stratagem. The perfect ploy to guarantee my win of the Yuletide Joust. A flawless gambit for me to become the future King of Finistère."

Chapter 11

Preparations for the Yuletide Joust

La Duchesse de Rohan sat in an ornately carved, blue velvet, tufted chair in the elegant antechamber of her royal quarters in *le Palais de la Cité* of Paris, sipping chamomile tea with her three female companions. Servants were packing their belongings in preparation for the upcoming voyage, when Béatrice would travel with the present trio of ladies to the oceanfront kingdom of Finistère to attend the Yuletide Joust. Pensively sipping her *tisane,* Gabrielle's great-aunt listened attentively to the court gossip her acquaintances were breathlessly eager to share.

Pinched face white with powdered pomade, Agnès—*la Marquise de Josselin*—remarked with scandalous delight, "The entire court is ablaze with the news of the attempted abduction of Princess Gabrielle. Imagine, armed men swooping out of the forest like hawks on horseback to ferret her away!"

Françoise, the rotund *Comtesse de Ploudry*, adjusted the strained seams of her pink satin gown. "And to think that the Master of Horse defended her against such an army! It is most fortunate that your nephew King Guillemin appointed him as her royal personal guard, Béatrice."

"Indeed," Béatrice agreed, setting her teacup down

on the lace-covered table. "Sir Bastien de Landuc is not only a most capable horseman, but a superior swordsman as well. It is most fitting that the king should reward such valor with a fiefdom, a castle, and *la noblesse chevaleresque*." She smiled proudly at Françoise. "Perhaps Sir Bastien de Landuc, the newly titled *Marquis de Cornouaille*, will win the Yuletide Joust. And Princess Gabrielle's hand in marriage." Béatrice smoothed her blue gown, slanting a covert glance at Clothilde, *la Vicomtesse de Vannes*, whose disdainful countenance clearly displayed her dissenting opinion of the matter.

La Vicomtesse clutched her porcelain teacup with skeletal claws, her dark, cunning eyes glinting with gleeful malice. "That, dear Béatrice, will never happen." Clothilde grinned wickedly, like a clever cat who had just snared an unsuspecting mouse.

Agnès, eager to impart her most impressive point of view, quipped enthusiastically: "He might very well triumph in the tournament, Clothilde. Rumor has it that Bastien de Landuc was trained by the legendary *Lancelot du Lac*, the greatest jousting champion in the entire realm." The pointed little teeth of her insincere smile yellowed in contrast with her artificially whitened *visage* as she haughtily observed the vicious *vicomtesse*.

A corner of Clothilde's thin, pursed mouth curved upward in a sardonic smirk, her gaunt cheeks wrinkling like crinkled parchment paper. "Bastien de Landuc will never win the Yuletide Joust. Ugolin le Clou has made certain of that." She sipped her tea with smug satisfaction while her noble counterparts shared curious, surprised glances.

"Whatever do you mean, dear Clothilde?" Françoise

exhaled excitedly, salivating at the salacious tidbit. "King Guillemin sent the royal *lettres patentes* last week. It is certain the *Parlement de Paris* has sanctioned the document and returned the approved, official decree to *le Château de Beaufort.* With plenty of time for Sir Bastien to qualify as a contestant in the Yuletide Joust."

La Vicomtesse de Vannes could scarcely contain herself. "King Guillemin's proclamation never reached *le Parlement de Paris."* The harpy leaned back in her tufted chair, a sanguine serpent confident of the vigor of its venom. "My husband's men intercepted that missive en route to Paris." She savored the tea sweetened by the sting of her waspish words, gloating with pernicious pleasure. "Even if Sir Bastien de Landuc were indeed capable of claiming victory in the Yuletide Joust, Ugolin le Clou will prevent him from entering the competition. He'll insist on documentation of Sir Bastien's nobility, which King Guillemin will be unable to provide. Sir Bastien will be ridiculed and disqualified as a mere knight impersonating a titled nobleman. A candidate unworthy of Princess Gabrielle's royal hand." Clothilde positively purred. "Ugolin le Clou shall triumph, as always. He shall win the Yuletide Joust. Marry the beautiful princess. And be crowned the King of Finistère."

Béatrice nearly choked on her tisane. *Clothilde's husband intercepted Guillemin's lettres patentes? The document never reached King Philippe or le Parlement de Paris?* She had to act quickly. The Yuletide Joust would begin in seven days. Béatrice knew how much her great-niece adored the handsome Bastien de Landuc. And how the magnificent Master of Horse at *le Château de Beaufort* loved the emerald-eyed, flame-haired

Gabrielle. She had to get an urgent message to her nephew.

Before it was too late.

Rising from her velvet tufted chair, her hand protectively clutching her abdomen, Béatrice whimpered as if in pain. "Please excuse me, *mes chères,* but I must visit the garderobe. Perhaps the tisane disagreed with me." She motioned for an attendant to serve the sumptuous pastries she had ordered from the palace kitchen. "In the meantime, please enjoy *les pâtisseries.* I'll return shortly."

Feigning stomach distress, Béatrice slipped from the parlor and darted down the long hall where embroidered tapestries decorated the wooden walls. Spotting an attendant waiting outside the door to an empty parlor, she beckoned the obedient servant to follow as she slid inside. "Fetch me parchment paper, a quill and ink, and wax to seal the document. Order a royal messenger to saddle a horse for immediate departure. Be discreet. The *communiqué* is confidential. No one must see him leave."

Eyes widened in wonder, the reliable attendant nodded earnestly and bowed with reverence. "*Oui, Madame la Duchesse. À vos ordres.*"

Several minutes later, the flustered valet returned with the requested items and the royal messenger. Leaning over a marble topped gilded table, Béatrice quickly penned a message, sealing the document and embossing the wax with her signet ring. She handed the scroll to the trusted envoy who had accompanied the valet. "Deliver this personally to King Guillemin of Finistère. Ride hard, change horses as necessary." Béatrice placed a bag of silver in the messenger's gloved hand. "This missive must reach the king within two days. Return to Paris with the document he will entrust in your care. I shall compensate you handsomely for your diligence and discretion. Depart at once."

"*Oui, Madame la Duchesse.* You have my solemn vow." The messenger tucked the scroll safely inside the leather pouch strapped across his torso, bowed in *obéisance* before Béatrice, and swiftly slipped down the stone stairs to the lower level of the palace.

"Mention this to no one." Béatrice placed several silver coins into the valet's palm, wrapping his fingers over the small fortune.

"I give you my word, *Madame la Duchesse,"* the servant murmured breathlessly. "Thank you for your generosity."

Béatrice ducked her chin in acknowledgement and strode down the hall toward the antechamber where her trio of traveling companions anticipated her return. At the entrance door, she inhaled deeply to regain her composure.

And whispered a silent prayer that her nephew Guillemin would receive the urgent message in time.

****

One week after the attempted abduction of Princess Gabrielle, Bastien's father, Sir Esclados le Ros, arrived at *le Château de Beaufort* with two dozen knights from Landuc, several grooms, and twenty magnificent Friesian and Ardennes horses for the Yuletide Joust. Accompanying Sir Esclados and his entourage were ten-year-old stable hand Quentin and his younger companion Gaston, thrilled to be involved in caring for the destriers and overjoyed at the prospect of meeting the legendary *Lancelot du Lac*, expected to arrive the following day.

Bastien greeted his father and the knights from Landuc, recognizing several soldiers from his family's castle in the Forest of Brocéliande. "Welcome to Beaufort. King Guillemin will greatly appreciate the extra defense of the castle for the Yuletide Joust."

"Several of my knights will be also participating in the opening events, hoping to earn a lady's favor." Esclados grinned at two of his knights atop their mounts. "Arnoulf and Didier—recently knighted at *le Château de Landuc*—are anxious to display their impressive chivalrous skills." Chuckling as he dismounted his own stallion, the Red Knight clasped Bastien's shoulders affectionately. "Congratulations on your title of nobility, son. Your mother and I received your message several days ago. We're both extremely proud and delighted that now, as *le Marquis de Cornouaille,* you're eligible to compete in the Yuletide Joust," Esclados boomed exuberantly, wrapping a chiseled arm around Bastien's neck in a congratulatory paternal embrace.

"Goddess willing, I'll win Gabrielle's hand. Nothing would give me greater joy." Bastien returned his father's expansive grin, then pivoted to welcome the two eager-faced young boys—atop their palfreys—whose eyes widened in wonder as they took in the bustling activity of ongoing joust preparations across the castle grounds. "It's good to see you both again, Quentin and Gaston. We'll certainly need your help caring for all the horses."

Esclados stroked the muzzle of the older boy's black Friesian. "Quentin is an exceptionally good stable hand. I'm grooming him to become Master of Horse at Landuc once he becomes a knight. Just as you did here at *le Château de Beaufort*, Bastien." His dark eyes alit with holiday joy, Esclados glanced at Gaston, then met Bastien's gaze, the two men smiling at the shared knowledge of Lancelot's intended Yuletide gift. Like Bastien and Quentin, young Gaston was also destined to become a groom, squire, and eventual knight. Under the peerless tutelage of his legendary hero, the great *Lancelot du Lac,* who would make Gaston's dreams come true when he appointed the boy as his personal squire to begin training in King Arthur's glorious castle of Camelot.

Bastien grinned at his father with jubilant holiday anticipation, imagining seven-year-old Gaston's unbridled joy as his greatest Yuletide wish came true. With a hearty chuckle. Bastien said cheerfully, "Boys, I'd like you to meet Maxence, my personal squire—and most trusted groom."

Upon this introduction, a tall, strapping youth of sixteen with sandy, shoulder-length hair, twinkling eyes, enormous shoulders, and a quiet, gentle disposition ducked his bristled chin with a wide smile. "Pleased to meet you, Quentin and Gaston. You can call me Max."

Clearly awestruck to meet the much older, most impressive squire, the two boys, still astride their mounts, eagerly shook hands with a grinning Max, who had walked over to greet them.

The still-smiling Max mounted his own horse, prepared to follow his *maître*, Sir Bastien de Landuc.

With effortless grace, Bastien hoisted himself into the saddle and announced to the group, "This way. I'll show you where we'll be staying." He escorted his father, the knights from Landuc, Max, the two boys, and the mounted grooms—leading the additional *destriers*—across the castle courtyard to the designated area where they would all be sheltered in tents for the duration of the joust.

They passed brightly color banners fluttering in the crisp December breeze as castle workers assembled pavilions along one side of the castle grounds for noble guests, opposite the lists where the tournament would take place. On the other side of the field, tents were being erected to shelter the competitors, their squires, grooms, and horses.

Carpenters were constructing the *berfrois* grandstand where visiting royalty and the highest-ranking nobles would receive preferential seating. And, closest to the castle itself was the magnificent, opulent wedding pavilion, being decorated with boughs of holly embellished with bright red berries and evergreen garlands interwoven with fragrant white hellebore blossoms.

Bastien's heart lurched at the sight of the white silk gazebo where he hoped to wed the woman he loved in six short days.

His flame-haired, fire-hearted Valkyrie.

The beautiful Gabrielle, his Viking Princess of Finistère.

He cast aside his pleasant, amorous reverie when they arrived at their destination. "This is where we'll be staying, along with the rest of the competitors." Bastien indicated a row of approximately a hundred tents, arranged into smaller, circular clusters. "Each competitor is assigned a group of tents for his grooms, squire, and horses. This area is ours." He dismounted, and the rest of the riders followed his example.

Castle cooks and servants were preparing food nearby over open fires in eating areas designated for the competitors, squires, and grooms to share meals. The tantalizing aroma of roasted meats and sizzling sausages wafted in the salty ocean breeze.

Noting the boys' hungry expressions as they ogled the appetizing food, Bastien said reassuringly, "You'll be able to get something to eat in just a few minutes, after we get settled in."

To Quentin and Gaston, he explained as he gestured to the area delineated for the competition, "The opening day ceremony, *les commençailles,* will take place here on the fourteenth. Some of the younger knights and squires will compete in three rounds of events—the lance, the sword, and the dagger. There'll be two intermissions, with theatrical performances, acrobats, and musicians. Those pavilions are designated for the entertainers," he informed them, indicating an array of vividly colored silk tents.

Pointing to the grandstand being built for preferred seating of the most prestigious nobles, Bastien announced, "That's where King Guillemin and Princess Gabrielle will watch the Yuletide Joust, along with my mother Laudine, Lancelot's mother—the Lady Viviane—and Gaston's mother, the Lady Ghislaine." He grinned at the beaming face of the young boy who was obviously proud that his beloved *Maman* would be seated near the King of Finistère. Bastien added with a reverent smile, "Prince Kaherdin and Princess Gargeolaine of *le Château Rose* in Armorique will be royal spectators as well."

Bastien gestured to a long row of red silk tents assembled near the grandstand. "During the joust, food and refreshments will be sold there. Vendors are setting up displays to sell clothing, jewelry, weapons, leather goods…even horses."

Amid the frenetic preparations for the upcoming joust, the knights from Landuc began unpacking their horses and settling into their respective tents.

Bastien told Max and the boys, "You three are sharing a tent with me. Get unpacked and settled in. Tend to the horses. And boys…" he said sternly, beckoning the trio to approach for a private message, "…no one but you will care for Drach. Understood?"

While Quentin and Gaston nodded eagerly and innocently, Max held Bastien's solemn gaze. *He understands the hidden message. Someone might try to poison my horse. A shadow sent by Ugolin le Clou.*

"You have my solemn vow. One of us will always be with Drach." Loyalty, integrity, and trust blazed in Max's brilliant blue eyes. "I give you my word, my lord."

While the boys scurried off with Max to tend to the horses and sample the delicious roasted meats, Esclados informed Bastien with a chuckle, "Gaspard will be escorting a trio of mothers—your own, Gaston's mother Ghislaine, and Lancelot's mother Viviane. He and a dozen knights from Landuc will travel by coach and arrive the day after tomorrow, on the twelfth."

Bastien watched with amusement as Max showed Gaston and Quentin how to properly groom Drach, the spirited black stallion nickering in equine pleasure under the combined ministrations of the three boys. Responding to his father's comment, Bastien remarked, "I've arranged accommodations—with adjacent rooms for the attendants—on the second floor of the castle. Guest chambers for Ghislaine and Gaspard, a lovely room for the Lady Viviane, and private quarters for you and *Maman*."

"We'll leave the rooms for the women and their servants. Gaspard and I plan to share tents with you and the boys. Lancelot and I are running the joust for King Guillemin, so it'll be much more convenient for us to be here near the lists with you. Gaspard can keep an eye on Quentin and Gaston. And I'll have several knights from Landuc guard our three women throughout the joust." Esclados scanned the row of tents. "Has Ugolin le Clou arrived?"

"Not yet, but he'll be staying over there." Bastien indicated an arrangement of five tents where banners displaying the distinctive cog ship and ermine symbols—the coat of arms of the seaport of Nantes—flapped in the crisp saline breeze. Glancing around to be sure no one could eavesdrop, he lowered his voice and locked eyes with his father. "Gabrielle believes that the royal physician Isnard is poisoning the king. No one has seen or heard from the healer in days—it's likely that he learned of her suspicions and disappeared before he could be apprehended." He stared at the flags fluttering over Ugolin's designated tents. "I think Ugolin le Clou placed him here. To slowly poison King Guillemin, forcing a hasty marriage for Gabrielle. With his father, le Marquis de Nantes, allied with the pirate Balthazar, Ugolin was confident that the implied threat of an attack would force King Guillemin to accept his request for Gabrielle's hand."

Bastien held his father's shrewd gaze. "Gabrielle retained one of Isnard's foul elixirs for Viviane, Ghilsaine, and *Maman* to analyze. She hopes they can identify the herbs and cleanse the king of any accumulated toxins. She also hopes that they might suggest alternative treatments for her father's ailments. She and I are both grateful that three renowned priestesses, skilled in herbal medicine, are coming to Finistère for the Yuletide Joust. If Gabrielle's suspicions prove true, Isnard will be charged with attempting to murder the king." He watched the cog ship—the symbol of Nantes, crucial seaport and hub of all shipping trade at the mouth of the Loire River—float on the winter wind as if on the open ocean. A vivid reminder of why Ugolin le Clou and his father Robert Cauchon were desperate to obtain the kingdom of Finistère.

To eliminate *le Traîté Maritime*.

And rule the Breton seas.

Bastien shuddered at the thought of Ugolin le Clou becoming King of Finistère. Not only would Ugolin control all shipping on the French coastline from the Loire Valley to the River Seine, he would also become Gabrielle's husband. An intolerable outcome that Bastien could never allow. He was determined to win the joust. Wed Gabrielle. And save Finistère.

Esclados' eyebrows furrowed into a pensive scowl. "A suspected poisoning of the king. An attempted abduction of the princess." Warning blazed in Esclados' warrior eyes. "Ugolin le Clou is behind both. And he'll act again. He'll try to win the Yuletide Joust at any cost. Have his champion charge with a sharpened lance. Slash your horse. Strive for a killing blow. He won't abide by the chivalrous rules of conduct outlined by the Statute of Arms for regulating jousts. He has no honor, son. Be on your guard at all times." Esclados scanned the competitors' tents, his scrutinizing gaze roving over the tournament field where the two jousting lanes were separated by ropes to prevent collision of the challengers. Nodding as if arriving at a crucial decision, Esclados announced wryly, "Lancelot and I will inspect all weapons before each and every run." His dark eyes blazed with protective, paternal fury. "Ugolin's champion, the Black Knight Sir Tréguier, will joust with the required blunted lance. Or be disqualified from the competition."

Bastien took a deep breath and exhaled slowly. "I hope I'm not disqualified from the competition either." His father raised an inquisitive eyebrow. "King Guillemin's royal messenger has not yet returned with the official decree from Parliament. Pray that he does within the week--before the joust begins." He sighed again and glanced at the turrets of the castle. "I must go now, to relieve Cardin. He's temporarily taken my place as Gabrielle's royal guard so that I could come and greet you. He'll be the one to protect her while I'm—Goddess willing—competing in the joust. And Gaultier, as First Knight of Beaufort, will guard the king."

An ominous chill rippled up Bastien's spine as a warning--a warrior's instinct-- niggled at the back of his mind. He locked eyes with his father. "When Lancelot arrives tomorrow, there's something important I want to show you, the knights of Landuc, and Lancelot's men from *la Joyeuse Garde*. I've already shown Gaultier, Cardin, King Guillemin, and our own knights of Beaufort." He spat on the ground and wiped his mouth with the back of his sleeve. "Inside the castle, there's a hidden trapdoor in the floor of the storage pantry—near the servants' exit. It leads down under the foundation of the *château* into a secret tunnel. To the west, it empties into a sea cave on the beach. And to the east, it leads up into the forest behind the castle, near *le Lac de Poulinoc*.

That's how I was able to save Gabrielle from being abducted. And it might be important in defending the castle. If, as you suspect, Ugolin le Clou does indeed act again."

With a hearty farewell and a promise to see them later that evening, Bastien left his father, the three boys, and the knights of Landuc to settle into the tents and groom the horses. And feast on the delectable roasted meats.

Inside the castle, Gaultier stood at attention, guarding the entrance to King Guillemin's private chambers with three other armored knights.

Bastien approached his older brother who acknowledged him with an affectionate fraternal smile. "How is the king?"

Gaultier's grave expression was sufficient response. "Not well. His stomach pains him, and his gout-swollen foot is excruciating. He's resting now." After a pause, he asked, "Has Father arrived with the horses and knights of Landuc?"

"Yes, I've just left them on the tournament field. They're unpacking…settling into the tents. Several of the knights are competing in *les commencçailles*—they've brought a dozen Friesian for the joust. And eight magnificent Ardennes. Quentin and Gaston are with them. I introduced the boys to Max. They'll take excellent care of Drach. And ensure he's never left unattended."

"Wise decision. With Ugolin le Clou's reputation for treachery, it's best to be prepared."

Bastien nodded. "Has the royal messenger returned from Paris?"

Apprehension reflecting in his dark eyes, Gaultier

averted his gaze. "Not yet."

The messenger was expected days ago. Delivering the royal decree from Paris which authenticated Bastien's newly appointed title of *le Marquis de Cornouaille*. Documenting his eligibility to compete in the Yuletide Joust. Bastien swallowed the tight knot constricting his throat. "I'm going to relieve Cardin now. He's been guarding Gabrielle while I welcomed Father and the knights of Landuc. Your replacements will arrive soon, so you can head out to the lists and greet them all. I'll see you later tonight." With a firm handshake and a nod to the other knights, Bastien left Gaultier and the king's royal guards.

He took the stone steps up to the second story of the castle, where his younger brother Cardin and a knight named Jeffroi guarded the entrance to Gabrielle's private chambers. "I've come to relieve you both," Bastien announced with a grin. "Thank you for your loyal service, Jeffroi."

The younger knight fisted his chest, ducked his chin, and left the two chivalrous brothers standing in front of the ornately carved wooden door.

Bastien informed Cardin, "Father and his knights just arrived. They're on the tournament field, unpacking the horses, getting established in the tents. Head on out to greet them and let me know when Lancelot arrives tomorrow. I want to take him and Father into the tunnel that I showed you and Gaultier—with the passages leading to the cave on the beach or the forest behind the castle near the lake. With Ugolin le Clou and his men attending the joust, I want a regiment of knights hidden in each position. To defend the castle, in the event he's planned a surprise attack."

Dark eyebrows furrowed in a pensive scowl, Cardin replied, “I’ll position soldiers as well—in strategic locations around the perimeter of the castle.” Battle experience blazing in his solemn gaze, he added, “Prince Kaherdin is arriving tomorrow with a bevy of armored knights from Armorique, wielding magnificent Elven weapons. With Kaherdin’s warriors, Lancelot’s soldiers, Father’s men from Landuc, and our own knights of Beaufort, we’ll be well defended on the tournament field. Gaultier and I will protect the king and Princess Gabrielle in the grandstand while you’re competing. And—with knights traveling through the tunnels to hide in defensive locations around the castle—we’ll be ready to counter any potential attack.”

With a firm handshake and a grin of agreement, Cardin bid his brother farewell and departed while Bastien knocked upon the carved golden oak door.

The white wimple of a humble servant appeared in the doorway. Bastien spotted Gabrielle seated at a table near the window. Her whole face alit in a dazzling smile as her eyes locked with his, she dismissed her attendant.

And welcomed him in.

Closing and bolting the door, she threw her arms around his neck, pulled his face down to hers, and placed her warm, inviting lips upon his. “Thank the Goddess, you’re here. I have missed you so…” She planted seductive kisses along his neck, nestling her nose into the dark hair protruding from his chest plate.

Emerald eyes ablaze, she looked up at him expectantly. Invitingly. Irresistibly.

Pulling her against him, his lips devoured hers, parting them with a probing, possessive tongue.

Gabrielle emitted a throaty moan and melted in his

arms.

He unlaced her bodice, lavished her lush breasts with warm, greedy lips, easing her gown and shift down over her shoulders to puddle on the floor.

Nude, trembling with desire, she stood before him, watching with parted lips and shallow breath as he threw off his armor and boots, dropped his scabbard and sword, and flung his breeches onto the wooden floor.

In a flash, he was upon her, his ardor unleashed. He wrapped her in his shaking arms, pressing his hardened body against hers as his mouth caressed her quivering flesh. He laid her upon the downy soft mattress of the feather bed, climbing over her, his heart slamming in his throat. Lowering his lips to hers, he traced and parted them with his tongue. His hungry mouth sought her white throat, her shoulders, suckling delicate pink nipples as enticing and sweet as nectar. Trailing kisses down her stomach, he tasted her luscious depths, his tongue probing and lips caressing the soft, tender flesh.

Writhing in pleasure, she begged, "Please, Bastien, I want you inside me."

With a guttural groan, he positioned himself between her quavering legs, parted her thighs with muscular knees, and slipped his hands under her soft, full hips. He tilted her pelvis up to receive him. And plunged into paradise.

A while later, they lay together, limbs entwined, bodies sated. He lovingly stroked the long red tresses as Gabrielle rested her head over his pounding heart. "I love you," he whispered, kissing her rose-scented hair. "To the very depths of my soul. I am yours, Gabrielle. Now and always."

"And I am yours, Bastien de Landuc." She buried

her nose into the dark hair on his chest, inhaling deeply as if to embed his scent into her very soul. "Totally, utterly, and completely yours." Raising herself up onto one elbow, she caressed his chest with her free hand, twirling the hair into little peaks and brushing them out again. She raised a crumpled face to his. "I simply cannot become another man's wife," she choked, her voice breaking. "Be forced to submit to him. Endure anyone but you inside my body." She shuddered violently and locked desperate eyes on his. "You *must* win the joust, Bastien. I cannot belong to anyone else."

He thought again of the delayed royal messenger. Without proof of a title of nobility, Bastien would be excluded from competing in the joust. The thought of Ugolin le Clou wedding and bedding Gabrielle filled him with impotent, sickening rage. Bitter bile rose in his constricted throat.

"If… I must marry someone else…" she stammered, her voice a breathless whisper, her fearful eyes brimming with unshed tears, "…perhaps we could still be lovers. When my husband is away…"

He pulled her possessively to his chest, cradling her upon his heaving heart. He would never risk her life for the pleasure of being her paramour. His own life, willingly. But hers…never. No, if she were forced to marry another, he would become a *chevalier itinérant*—a knight errant. He'd offer the service of his sword in a distant, foreign kingdom.

Far from Finistère.

For he could never bear to see her in another man's arms. Or endure the thought of another man between her long, lithe legs. He shuddered with jealous revulsion.

"Shhh," he murmured, stroking her tousled hair.

"There's still time for the royal messenger to arrive from Paris. The joust begins in three days. Goddess willing, your father will receive the decree from *le Parlement* in time for me to compete. We must keep the faith, my love. I shall win your hand. And you, my flame-haired, fire-hearted Valkyrie, will be my wedded wife. Now, come here. Let me show you how much I love you."

With a whimper of willing acquiescence, fragile hope, and unbridled desire, Gabrielle succumbed.

And Bastien lavished her—body and soul—with all the love and lust in his fierce Breton heart.

Chapter 12

Les Arrivées

The following day, Lancelot arrived with two dozen knights from *la Joyeuse Garde* and a dozen prized warhorses for the Yuletide Joust. Bastien, his father Esclados, and the knights of Landuc greeted the entourage with a hearty welcome on the tournament field near the lists. Today, Gaultier—the First Knight of Beaufort—was among them, having assigned royal guards to assist Cardin with defending King Guillemin and Princess Gabrielle.

Since Maxence, as Bastien's squire, already knew Lancelot well from the summers spent with his lord at *la Joyeuse Garde*, he led the knights and grooms toward the assigned tents to unpack and tend to the horses while Bastien introduced the two remaining awestruck boys to his formidable former mentor.

"May I present Sir *Lancelot du Lac,"* Bastien exclaimed heartily. "First Knight of Camelot and Champion of King Arthur Pendragon. The lord who trained me each summer at his glorious castle, *la Joyeuse Garde.* The legendary knight whose equestrian lessons enabled me to become Master of Horse for King Guillemin." He grinned at Lancelot, who dismounted from an enormous black stallion to stand proudly before the enthralled youths. "The unparalleled horseman who gave me Drach, my magnificent Percheron, when I became a knight here at *le Château de Beaufort*."

Adulation stretching across his freckled face, Quentin beamed with pride when Bastien remarked affably to Lancelot, "This is Quentin, my father's best stable hand. In fact, Lord Esclados is grooming him to become Master of Horse at Landuc."

Tossing his dark, wavy hair behind his broad shoulders, Lancelot offered an outstretched hand as he flashed Quentin a dazzling grin. In a rich, deep baritone, he boomed, "Pleased to make your acquaintance, Quentin. I'm always glad to meet a fellow horseman."

Young Gaston lingered shyly behind Quentin, his limpid blue eyes widened in wonder as he stared open-mouthed at Lancelot, the hero he worshipped like a god. The idol who would make the boy's dreams come true with his incredible Yuletide gift.

Bastien motioned for Gaston to approach.

His chin ducked, a timid smile breaking across his wonderstruck face, Gaston sauntered up to Bastien.

To meet the renowned Lancelot of the Lake.

"This is Gaston—Ghislaine and Gaspard's son. My squire Max and Quentin are teaching him to groom the horses, too. He's been a tremendous help, caring for my stallion Drach." Bastien chuckled at the boy's flushed, flustered face. "He's a natural, Sir Lancelot. Just like you and me."

Lancelot firmly but gently shook Gaston's small hand, then squatted down to look the lad directly in the eye. "I've heard a lot about you, Gaston. It's a pleasure to finally meet you at long last." Affection and pride shone in Lancelot's assessing gaze. Rising to his feet, he offered, "Would you like to meet my horse? His name is

Gosse, and he's a black Percheron, just like Drach." Taking Gaston by the hand, Lancelot led the boy toward the enormous horse, who nickered in greeting.

A few moments later, Gaston sat astride the massive charger, grinning from ear to ear, as Lancelot led his warhorse across the grassy courtyard. Returning to offer Quentin a ride as well, Bastien watched the bemused First Knight of Camelot entertain the two awestruck, astonished boys.

"Well, Gosse needs to be watered and groomed now, and so does Drach. How about you two take care of them for us, while Max and the stable hands groom the other horses? Curry their coats, clean their hooves…feed them some barley and oats. When you've finished, we'll head on over to see what the cooks have got sizzling over those open fires." He inhaled deeply, savoring the heady aroma. "Smells like roast boar. With honey. *Delicious*." With a hearty grin, he chuckled as the rapt boys dashed off, eager to obey.

Esclados, with Gaultier at his side, joined them as the two boys sped by. He grinned at Lancelot. "They certainly enjoyed riding your Percheron. He's a fine animal. I'll bet he's won you many a joust."

"Indeed, he has." Lancelot cast an admiring glance at his black stallion, preening under the adulation of the young, attentive grooms.

"Gaultier and I want to show you a hidden passage that I discovered inside the castle." Bastien grinned at his older brother, bemused by the looks of astonishment on their father's and Lancelot's intrigued faces. "There's a trap door in the floor of the storage room near the kitchen pantry. It opens into a tunnel under the foundation, leading west to a sea cave on the beach. Or east, to the forest behind the château, near *le Lac de Poulinoc*. Where Gaultier, Cardin, and I used to hunt as squires."

Bastien noticed several older grooms were working alongside Max, Quentin, and Gaston. "I'll be right back," he said to his companions as he strode over to speak to the young men and boys tending the horses. "I'm going inside the castle with Sir Gaultier, Sir Lancelot, and Sir Esclados. We'll be back soon," he told Max. "Keep an eye on the boys and the horses for us until we return." To Quentin and Gaston, he said, "Stay here with Max. We won't be long."

Max ducked his chin, respect and loyalty shining in his bright eyes. "Yes, my lord. We'll take good care of the horses and wait here for your return."

Brushes in hand as they curried the horses, the younger boys nodded in earnest agreement.

Bastien returned to Lancelot, Gaultier, and Esclados. With a tilt of his head, he said, "Come on, let's go."

Inside the castle, Bastien led Gaultier, their father, and Lancelot to the storage pantry near the servants' exit. He lit a torch taken from the wall sconce and handed it to his father as he unlocked and lifted the hidden trap door in the floor. "I'll go down first, and you can hand me the torch." He slipped through the opening, down into the dark, cavernous foundation under the castle within the cliff upon which the fortress was built.

Esclados gave Bastien the torch and slid down through the floor, followed by Lancelot, then Gaultier, who closed the trap door above his head.

The serpentine tunnel twisted into the darkness before them. "This way," Bastien said, illuminating the gloom with the torch held high.

Damp with mildew, the stone walls of the limestone cave were beaded with moisture, the saline scent of the sea permeating the rich, fecund scent of ancient soil and primordial rock. Through the winding twists and turns of the dark passage, they arrived at the mouth of the sea cave which opened onto the sandy shore. As they emerged from the grotto, sea gulls squawked in a pale winter sky scattered with thin white clouds under a mild hibernal sun.

Lancelot scanned the beach and the high forested ridge of the craggy cliff behind them. Spotting the narrow path leading from the shore to the top of the rocky precipice, he asked Bastien, "Is that how you saved Gabrielle? You rode to the ledge, came down this path, and up into the castle through the cave?"

"Exactly." Bastien indicated the edge of the forest at the top of the cliff. "Just south of here is the open moor where we always trained with swords. That's where the attempted abduction occurred."

Esclados walked across the sandy beach to join them in examining the forested ledge. "If the castle were ever compromised, a regiment of men could slip through the cave, up this path, and position themselves behind any attackers. Although horses could never fit through the tunnel, the castle archers could take out any invaders with a surprise rear attack from the south."

Bastien eyed his companions. His esteemed father, the Red Knight Esclados le Ros. Lord of *le Château de Beaufort* and battle-seasoned warrior. His older brother Gaultier, the First Knight of Beaufort. Champion to King Guillemin of Finistère. And his former mentor Lancelot, the intrepid First Knight of King Arthur Pendragon. Unparalleled with the sword and peerless in the saddle.

Highly respected knights who would officiate the Yuletide Joust. Seasoned warriors who would defend the castle with prowess, courage, and skill. Bastien exhaled a sigh of relief. "Indeed. Come, I'll show you where the tunnel leads to the east. Another strategic position for defense."

Dappled sunlight glimmered on the rippled surface of *le Lac de Poulinoc* through the dense foliage of massive oak, beech, and fir trees as they exited the woodland cave. The fresh tang of the lake mingled with the briny saline breeze of the nearby ocean and the crisp green scent of pine.

"We're about a half mile behind the castle," Bastien informed the men who inspected the surrounding forest with the keen eyes of experienced commanders.

"We'll position a regiment of archers here, to the east," Gaultier announced, indicating a hamlet of dense oaks with low lying branches.

"And place another contingent in the heavy woods there, to the north." Lancelot extended an arm toward the designated thick forest.

"In addition to a hundred armored knights waiting inside the castle, with orders to reinforce each location in the event of attack." Esclados—who had successfully defended his own castle, *le Château de Landuc,* through several such sieges—offered his prudent proposition.

"Given Ugolin le Clou's reputation for refusing to concede any loss, and the fact that his champion is competing in the Yuletide Joust, it is best if we prepare for the worst." Bastien clasped his father's strong, sculpted shoulder. "I shall heed your sage advice."

"Let's return now. I promised a trio of famished boys that we'd sample the roast boar." Lancelot chuckled softly, his famous boyish grin illuminating his noble face.

Satisfied with their strategy to defend *le Château de Beaufort*, the four knights entered the cave, traversed the dark tunnel, and returned through the trap door to the storage pantry inside the castle kitchen.

As Bastien locked the door and replaced the rushes across the top to conceal the hidden passage in the floor, the clatter of carriage wheels and the clomping of horses' hooves from the front of the castle indicated that guests had begun to arrive.

Valets welcomed *les arrivées* while attendants unpacked the coaches for grooms to lead the horses toward the castle stables.

Spotting her auburn hair and cordial smile, Bastien rushed to greet his mother Laudine with the familiar French greeting of *la bise*—a kiss on each cheek.

"Oh, Bastien! I am delighted to see you, son!" Laudine wrapped her arms around his neck and smothered him in an affectionate maternal hug. "Congratulations on your title as *le Marquis de Cornouaille*. Your father and I are so very proud. And now, you may compete in the Yuletide Joust!"

Bastien held his effusive mother and smiled as he disengaged himself from her exuberant embrace. *If the royal messenger arrives in time, Maman.* He turned to welcome Gaston's parents, with a hearty handshake for Gaspard and a kiss on the cheek for Ghislaine.

Gaultier and Esclados kissed and welcomed Laudine, while Lancelot hugged his own mother, the Lady of the Lake, Viviane.

Amidst the affectionate greetings, Bastien spotted Gabrielle floating down the spiral stairs into the spacious foyer where evergreen boughs and garlands of fragrant Yuletide holly decorated the whitewashed walls. Candlelight from the crystal chandelier overhead blended with afternoon sunlight streaming in through the western windows overlooking the sea, casting her long red hair in a glorious golden blaze which took his breath away.

She rushed to accept his outstretched hand with a warm smile for the newly arrived guests, who bowed in *obéisance* before the Princess of Finistère.

"My princess, allow me to introduce my parents, Sir Esclados le Ros and the Lady Laudine of *le Château de Landuc* in the Forest of Brocéliande." Bastien beamed as his father gallantly kissed Gabrielle's slender white hand and his mother executed a graceful curtsey.

Affection and admiration shone in Gabrielle's expressive emerald eyes. "Welcome to *le Château de Beaufort*. It is a pleasure to meet you both."

"And this is the Lady of the Lake Viviane, High Priestess of Avalon and mother to the great *Lancelot du Lac*, whom you met a few months ago upon your return from Paris." Bastien introduced Gabrielle to the elegant lady who bowed before the princess as the chivalrous knight kissed her royal hand.

"I am honored to meet the esteemed Lady of the Lake, mother of the legendary *Lancelot du Lac*," Gabrielle said cordially as she greeted the famous mother and illustrious son.

"You are a gracious hostess, Princess Gabrielle. Thank you for the royal invitation and accommodations for us to attend the Yuletide Joust." Viviane turned to the humbled couple at her side. "May I present my dear friends Gaspard and Ghislaine of Brocéliande."

"*Enchantée*." Gabrielle smiled as Ghislaine curtseyed and Gaspard bowed reverently. "Please allow my attendants to show you to your rooms. I am sure you'd like to refresh after your long journey." She smiled hesitantly, concern reflecting in her verdant gaze. "My father is quite ill—otherwise, he would be here to greet you as well." She glanced nervously at Bastien. "Bastien informed me that you three priestesses are all gifted healers, exceptionally skilled with medicinal herbs." Gabrielle looked down at her feet, then raised imploring eyes toward the trio of women. "I hope you might be able to examine the king—and perhaps suggest a treatment which might assuage his pain and improve his ailing health. Perhaps this afternoon, after you've had a chance to rest, I might send a servant to escort you to his royal chambers?"

Viviane responded without hesitation. "Of course. We will be honored to examine and treat your father." She smiled knowingly at her two female companions. "We specialize in the healing arts and have our herbal supplies with us. Please, Princess Gabrielle, send an attendant in an hour. That will give us time to unpack our bags and refresh, so we'll be presentable to meet King Guillemin."

Esclados kissed his wife's cheek in parting. "The rooms in the castle, we men will leave to you ladies. Gaspard and I will be staying in the tents with Bastien and Lancelot down on the tournament field. He'll keep an eye on Gaston and Quentin while Lancelot and I officiate the competition. I've assigned several knights from Landuc to escort you to the opening ceremony tomorrow morning. *Les commençailles* begin at ten, so I'll have the guards report shortly after nine. I'll see you then, my love. *À demain.*"

Gaspard kissed his wife Ghislaine, and Lancelot bid adieu to his mother.

Tears of joy brimming in her proud amber eyes, Laudine kissed Bastien and murmured, "Good luck in the joust, son. My Yuletide wish is for you to win the tournament. And Princess Gabrielle's lovely hand."

Mine, too, Maman. If the royal decree arrives before tomorrow. Bastien brushed his lips against his mother's soft cheek and said to his father, "I'll stay here with Gabrielle while the healers assess King Guillemin. I'll come down to the field and join you later this evening." He waved goodbye as Lancelot, Esclados, Gaultier, and Gaspard exited the castle and headed back to the lists, while the trio of female priestesses followed the servants upstairs to their respective guest quarters.

Alone with Bastien in the empty foyer, her eyes alit with fragile hope, Gabrielle whispered, "I hope your mother, Viviane, and Ghislaine can identify the harmful herbs that Isnard was giving my father. Perhaps cleanse the toxins from his blood somehow. And offer a treatment for his stomach pain and excruciating gout." She watched the men retreat from view as they crossed the castle grounds, then turned to Bastien and suggested, "Let's share a small meal in my chambers before we bring the healers to meet my father. Come, I'll have something brought to my room."

Gabrielle opened the carved golden oak door of her elegant antechamber at the servant's knock. The attendant entered with an appetizing platter of cold meats, cheese, bread, and fruit, which he placed upon the table. Pouring two silver goblets from the elaborate decanter, he placed the remainder of the wine in the center of the sumptuous array and discreetly disappeared.

Tracing the decorative edge of the pewter platter, Gabrielle's pensive gaze fixed on the goblets of wine. When she raised her forlorn eyes, the fear and despair he glimpsed in their emerald depths pierced his heavy heart. "The messenger still has not arrived with the decree of *le Parlement de Paris*. And the opening ceremonies begin tomorrow."

Without authentication of his noble title, Bastien would not be permitted to compete in the Yuletide Joust. At the thought of Ugolin le Clou winning Gabrielle's hand, his throat constricted; he couldn't breathe. Clenching his jaw, he swallowed the bitter bile rising from his raging gut.

Gabrielle slipped across the room to stand before him, gentle fingers caressing the stubble on his cheek. "This might be the last time we're alone together."

He grasped her hand and turned an anguished face to kiss the inside of her palm, his breath ragged and rough.

She slid into his embrace, wrapping her other arm behind his neck, rising onto her toes to kiss the thundering pulse of his throat. "Please, Bastien…make love to me."

A jolt of desire shot through him like a bolt of lightning. Cradling her upturned, pleading face within his two calloused hands, he claimed her mouth with ravenous, possessive lips and probing, insistent tongue. The rosewater scent of her luxurious tresses filled his lungs with her intoxicating essence, her taste evoking waves of desire that crashed into him like the thunderous surf pounding against the cliff below the castle.

He unhooked her bodice, his clumsy fingers fumbling with the laces, his body straining, throbbing, and aching. Sliding the velvet down to expose her bare shoulders, he cupped her soft breasts, lapping and sucking the pert pink nipples as she moaned and swooned against him.

Bastien unstrapped his scabbard and dropped his sword, which clattered on the cold wooden floor. He threw off his armor, chemise, sabatons, and hose to stand naked, shaking with ardor, before his beautiful, flame-haired Valkyrie.

Nude, visibly trembling, she stepped out of the gown, which pooled on the floor as she slid toward him. Desire danced in her emerald eyes as her gaze rove hungrily over his aroused body. Her quavering hands caressed the dark hair on his chest, her swollen lips sampling the skin over his muscled torso.

A guttural groan poured from the back of his throat.

He pulled her supple body against his, his rough fingers caressing her smooth back and silky bottom, the sleek skin a sensuous delight against his hardened muscles and coarse hair. His ardent desire pressed firmly against her soft, yielding flesh, he eased her toward the bed and laid her down upon the edge, opening her soft, creamy thighs.

She wrapped long, lithe legs behind his waist, her arms around his tensed back, kissing and sucking his shoulders, pulling him deep into her welcoming warmth with desperate, impatient limbs.

His feet planted firmly on the floor, his hands cupped under her rounded hips, he pounded her until thunderous waves of pleasure crashed over them both as he filled her with his copious seed.

Legs shaking from the intensity of their passion, he crawled onto the bed and drew her into his protective embrace, showering her rose-scented tresses with soft, appreciative kisses.

She rested her head over his galloping heart, burying her nose in his chest hair as he smoothed her long, tousled mane. “I love you with all my heart, Bastien. I pray the royal messenger will arrive in time for you to win my hand. I will die… if I am given to another man.” Gabrielle kissed his chest, inhaling deeply, as If drawing his scent, his essence, into her lungs. “I want only you. Now…and forever. In my heart, I shall always be your wife. Even if I am wedded against my will to another.”

He brushed away a strand of hair stuck to her tear-stained cheek. Wrapping his hands behind her head, Bastien pulled her face to his, seeking her salty lips with his own.

Rising onto her knees, she straddled him, rubbing the silky flesh between her thighs against his thickening body. Tumbling tresses wrapped him in cascading flames as she parted his lips with her own and slipped her tender tongue inside.

Between her legs, his aroused body probed, seeking entrance, desperate for her luscious warmth. Gripping her hips, he pulled her down onto himself, moaning in relief with each powerful upward thrust. Soon, she collapsed onto his chest, convulsing in pleasure, extracting every drop of his seed as her body clamped upon his in the clenching contractions of climax.

His arms wrapped around her back, he held her against his chest and stroked her damp hair. “As much as I hate to leave this bed, we must get dressed. You promised to send an attendant to fetch my mother,

Ghislaine, and Viviane for them to examine your father."

Gabrielle rose, removed her legs from the straddled position over him, and sat down on the bed. She smoothed the hair away from her face. "Yes, I want to introduce them to Papa. Reassure him that they are gifted healers who mean to help." She stood up and collected her gown from the floor as Bastien donned his breeches and chemise, fastened his chest plate armor, and pulled a tunic over his head.

He eyed the appetizing food, the aroma of fresh bread, meat and cheese making his mouth water. "I'm famished. Let's eat before we go." He watched longingly as she tightened the laces of her bodice, his body stirring at the sight of the soft swell of her breasts. By the Goddess, he longed to devour them again…

Shaking his dark hair back down his shoulders, he dispelled the desire which threatened to throttle him and strode up to the table to prepare a plate for Gabrielle.

Her gown refastened, she smoothed her hair and declined the proffered food. "I can't eat. My stomach is in knots. But perhaps a goblet of wine…" She reached for the two chalices, handed one to Bastien, and swallowed a large gulp from her own.

He placed his chalice upon the table, took the goblet from her hand and set it down next to his. Pulling her onto his lap, he enveloped her in his adoring arms, kissing the side of her neck. "There's still time for the messenger to arrive. Let's have faith. And concentrate on healing your father." He reached for the nutty, grainy bread and tore off a chunk, offering it to her. "Now, eat something. For me."

A sad smile spread across her resigned face as she accepted the bread along with his words. "For you,

Bastien. Anything for you." She took a bite, chewed it slowly, and washed it down with more wine before rising to her feet and strolling to the window to gaze out at the turbulent sea. "*Le Traîté Maritime.* My father's proudest accomplishment." She turned toward him, anguish blazing in her emerald eyes. "I cannot marry Ugolin le Clou. He would revoke the treaty and gain control of all shipping on the Breton seas. My father's greatest achievement would be undone. His life's work ruined. And the kingdom of Finistère lost. I cannot allow that to happen. Bastien…what can we do?"

He walked across the room and took hold of her hands, raising them to his lips as he held her imploring gaze. "Pray that the messenger arrives in time. Come, let's eat. Go to your father. And send for the healers."

****

The afternoon sun, setting over the turquoise sea, cast soft rays of golden light through the large ogival windows, partially opened to allow a crisp, cleansing ocean breeze into the royal antechamber. His once-auburn hair now sparse and gray, his formerly robust, ruddy complexion now pale and wan, King Guillemin sat stiffly in the blue velvet tufted chair which served as an informal throne while Ezhvin, the loyal royal chamberlain, gently eased the king's grotesquely swollen, bare left foot onto an adjacent supportive chair. Fiery red and horribly inflamed, with an enormous yellow blister distended and ready to burst, the inflammation caused obvious, excruciating pain, for her father tightly gripped the ornately carved arms of golden oak, his face contorted in agony, as Gabrielle and Bastien entered the room and bowed before the King of Finistère.

Approaching from his right, Gabrielle kissed the

king's sunken cheek and knelt beside the throne, Bastien standing attentively at her side. "*Bonjour, Papa.*" She tenderly brushed a strand of stringy hair from the king's gaunt face. "Bastien's mother, the Lady Laudine, has arrived at Beaufort. With the Lady Viviane—Lancelot's mother and High Priestess of Avalon—and the Lady Ghislaine, a gifted healer from the Forest of Brocéliande." She looked up at Bastien, his fierce green eyes instilling her with hope and strength. "I have sent for them to come examine you. And this," she said, reaching for the stoppered vial that Bastien placed in her extended hand. "The elixir that Isnard served you the day I was abducted. Remember? "

She showed her father the small amber flask. "I saved it, for them to analyze. And perhaps suggest an alternative treatment." Gabrielle addressed Ezhvin, patiently attending the king near a carved walnut, marble-topped sideboard upon which a platter of wine and several goblets awaited the expected guests. "Please send for the three healers. We're ready to receive them now."

"*Oui, Votre Majesté.*" Ezhvin motioned to two valets who stood at attention near the double entrance doors.

At his command, the escorts bowed, departed, and returned a few minutes later with the trio of priestesses.

Bastien kissed his mother's cheeks in *la bise* of familiar greeting as Gabrielle welcomed Viviane and Ghislaine. "Thank you very much for coming. Allow me to introduce you to my father, King Guillemin." She approached her father's informal throne. "Papa, I'd like you to meet the three healers who have come to treat you. This is Bastien's mother, the Lady Laudine. Lancelot's mother, the Lady Viviane. And Lady Ghislaine, a priestess from the Forest of Brocéliande."

The three healers bowed in *obéisance* before the King of Finistère.

"A pleasure to meet you. Welcome to Finistère." Grimacing, his jaw tightly clenched, he indicated his swollen foot with a jut of his chin. "I hope you can alleviate the agony of my gout. The pain is unbearable."

Long black hair streaked with silver cascaded over her shoulders as Viviane lowered her head to examine the king's sickeningly bloated foot. "I have a remedy to ease the inflammation and reduce the swelling."

Gabrielle handed the stoppered vial to Bastien's mother Laudine. "This is the herbal treatment that the royal physician Isnard was giving my father. I suspect it has harmful herbs, because shortly after the healer began treating my father's gout, his symptoms not only worsened, but he was plagued with severe stomach pain, vomiting, and diarrhea." At her father's horrified look of embarrassment, she rubbed his shoulder and murmured, "It's all right, Papa. They're *healers*."

Laudine removed the stopper and sniffed the contents. "Cloying and sweet." She handed the vial to Viviane.

"Like honeysuckle," Viviane replied, waving the open flask under her nose. She passed the small flagon to Ghislaine, who smelled the contents and nodded in agreement before responding solemnly, "Deadly nightshade. Highly toxic."

"It causes stomach irritation, cramping, nausea, and vomiting. All the symptoms your father has been experiencing. A larger dose would have been fatal." Viviane replaced the stopper on the vial. "Fortunately, it can be cleansed from the body with burdock root and red clover." She smiled at Ezhvin. "Please send for a kettle of boiling water and a cup, that I may prepare King Guillemin an herbal cleansing *tisane.*"

"At once, my lady." The king's royal chamberlain spoke quietly to one of the valets, who quickly disappeared to obey.

Laudine strode over to the marble topped sideboard and placed her reticule of herbal supplies on top of the elaborate table, retrieving several small vials and pouches of dried herbs. "We'll prepare a *tisane* to cleanse your blood. And herbs to reduce inflammation and swelling caused by the gout, Your Majesty." Her amber eyes compassionate and kind, Laudine smiled sympathetically at the king. "The nightshade also aggravated your symptoms, so once all traces are eliminated from your body, they will greatly improve."

The valet returned with a steaming teapot and porcelain mug on a pewter platter, setting it upon the sideboard before Laudine and retreating to stand beside Ezhvin and the other male servant near the door.

"Cinnamon and dandelion extract will enhance the cleansing effects of the burdock root and red clover." With a small spoon she retrieved from her sack, Bastien's mother measured the herbs into the cup and poured boiling water to steep the *tisane.*

Ghislaine placed her sack of herbal supplies on a corner of the carved wooden sideboard near Laudine and removed several tiny vials. "Essential oils will reduce the inflammation of your gout, Your Highness. And relieve the excruciating pain." With careful, measured droplets, she blended the essence of herbal oils as the floral fragrance of lavender and the herbal scents of rosemary, chamomile, and thyme wafted into the fresh air. Gingerly, she applied a small amount of the curative oils on King Guillemin's badly swollen foot and with tender, delicate fingers, performed a light, soothing *effleurage.*

As Ghislaine's skilled hands gently massaged the fragrant oils into his distended foot, the king moaned in blessed relief, the grimace of pain easing the furrows in his haggard face.

"Tart cherry extract and ginger are also excellent for treating gout. I'll prepare a tincture for you to add to the king's tea," Viviane informed Gabrielle. "Give him the burdock root and red clover tea three times a day. Serve him a ginger and tart cherry tonic in the evening, a couple hours after his meal." To Ezhvin, she said with a smile, "Massage three drops of this essential oil into his swollen foot twice a day. He will feel immediate relief. As he has just now."

Gabrielle noted the profound look of relaxation on her father's face as he thanked Ghislaine for the gentle massage.

Laudine strained the herbs from the tea she had prepared, stirring the mixture with her spoon, releasing the sweet, spicy scent of cinnamon as she served the king his cleansing *tisane.*

He sipped the steaming herbal brew, basking in visible alleviation of pain and enjoying the solicitous attention of the three gifted healers. When he'd consumed every drop, he returned the empty cup to Laudine with a grateful smile. "The *tisane* was quite pleasant. Cinnamon adds a delightful flavor. Thank you, Lady Laudine." Exhaling in a sigh of solace, contentment glowing in his hazel eyes, he beheld Ghislaine, who had completed the foot massage and was wiping the essential oils from her hands with a linen cloth. "That was heavenly, Lady Ghislaine. Instant relief from the pain. I cannot thank you enough." He leaned back in his chair, eyelids lowered in obvious satisfaction. "Thank you all. I feel refreshed, relaxed, and rejuvenated. You are indeed most highly skilled." Comfort and profound relaxation evident in his assuaged features, King Guillemin said magnanimously, "Please join Gabrielle and me tonight in my solar, to share the evening meal as my most distinguished guests." He addressed Bastien with a hearty grin. "You and your brothers must attend, with Lancelot, Esclados, and the Lady Ghislaine's husband. What is his name, my lady?"

"Gaspard, Your Royal Highness. My husband and I are honored to accept your most gracious invitation. We humbly thank you, my king." Tendrils of soft brown curls escaped her lace wimple as Ghislaine bowed her head with reverence.

"We'll return to our quarters now, so that you may rest for a few hours, *Votre Majesté*." Viviane gave Gabrielle the ginger and tart cherry extract. "Prepare a tonic of this tincture for the king to imbibe each evening. It will reduce the inflammation and eliminate the toxins which cause gout."

Laudine handed her the herbs for his three daily cups of cleansing, curative tea. "Steep two teaspoons of this mixture in boiling water for five minutes before straining the herbs. Have your father drink the *tisane* three times daily for the next two weeks to remove all traces of the deadly nightshade that the royal physician administered." She squeezed Gabrielle's hand, hope shining in amber eyes gilded in the golden sunlight.

Ghislaine entrusted the essential oils to Ezhvin for

the king's twice daily foot massage.

And, amid heartfelt expressions of gratitude and fond farewells, the three healers packed up their herbal supplies, bowed before the king, kissed Gabriellc and Bastien with *la bise* on each cheek, and returned to their respective chambers until the evening meal.

Gabrielle walked to the side of her father's informal throne and clasped his weathered hand. Tears of gratitude filled her eyes as she leaned down to kiss his relaxed cheek. "I am so grateful they were able to alleviate your pain." She eased a stray lock of gray hair away from his thick brow. "The herbs can cleanse all the toxins from your blood. Every trace of Isnard's poison." She dropped to her knees and rested her head on his shoulder. "They will make you well again, Papa. Thank the Goddess…"

As King Guillemin lovingly stroked her long red hair, a servant appeared in the doorway. "Forgive the intrusion, Your Majesty, but *la Duchesse de Rohan* has just arrived and has requested a royal audience."

Gabrielle lifted her head and grinned at her father as she jumped to her feet. "*Tatie* is here!"

The king repositioned himself and addressed the awaiting attendant. "Show her in."

Ezhvin discreetly placed a velvet tufted armchair beside the king as Gabrielle's great-aunt swept into the room in wafting waves of turquoise silk and pristine white ermine fur.

"Guillemin! How good it is to see you again. It has been far too long." As Béatrice floated across the room to grace her nephew's cheeks with *la bise* of greeting, her two meek female attendants took their places beside Ezhvin and the valet near the carved walnut, green marble top sideboard table.

Her expressive brown eyes twinkling in the afternoon setting sun, *la Duchesse de Rohan* positively beamed at Gabrielle as she enthusiastically clasped her great-niece's hands and thoroughly assessed her with admiration and genuine affection. "Ah, *chérie,* how I have missed you! And how beautiful you are in this most becoming color of deepest green." Béatrice kissed her lovingly on each cheek.

Gabrielle smiled as she smoothed her gown and reached for Bastien's hand, pulling him to her side for the introduction. "*Tatie,* I'd like you to meet Sir Bastien de Landuc. Master of Horse here at *le Château de Beaufort.* My equestrian and weaponry instructor. The personal royal guard who defended me when armed horsemen attacked and attempted to abduct me." Hoping he could see the lovelight in her adoring eyes, Gabrielle whispered as she gazed at Bastien, "He saved my life, *Tatie*."

With chivalrous panache, Bastien lowered his head to bestow a gallant kiss upon Béatrice's elegantly ringed hand.

"A noble, heroic deed for which I appointed him *le Marquis de Cornouaille."* King Guillemin twisted awkwardly in his tufted throne to address his sophisticated aunt. "However, we have yet to receive the official decree from *le Parlement de Paris* authenticating his newly bestowed title."

Ezhvin ushered *la Duchesse de Rohan* to the blue velvet tufted chair near a small table at the king's side. Attentive valets seated Gabrielle and Bastien next to Béatrice and poured goblets of fine French wine for King Guillemin and his royal guests.

While everyone sampled the fruity *bordeaux,* Béatrice retrieved something from the silk reticule at her feet. With a triumphant grin, she handed her nephew a rolled parchment tied with black silk ribbon and sealed with embossed red wax.

At his look of bewilderment, *la Duchesse de Rohan* grinned mischievously, one perfect eyebrow raised in impish delight. "The official decree from *le Parlement de Paris*. Documenting Sir Bastien de Landuc as *le Marquis de Cornouaille*."

Gabrielle's mouth dropped open in a breathless gasp. She glanced at Bastien, whose eyes were widened in astonishment.

And unbridled joy.

"I am truly grateful that the message I sent reached you in time, Guillemin." Béatrice leaned forward in her chair, smiling reassuringly at an astounded Gabrielle. "Your father's original decree was intercepted en route to Paris by a close ally of Ugolin le Clou. Fortunately, my friend Clothilde—wife of *le Vicomte de Vannes* who seized the royal proclamation—so desperately enjoys sharing scandalous gossip that she revealed her husband's subterfuge. I, of course, dispatched an immediate envoy to Finistère, with orders for him to return to Paris with your father's response—a duplicate decree of *la noblesse chevaleresque* for Sir Bastien de Landuc." Béatrice grinned, her soft cheeks crinkling with youthful glee. "I paid my royal messenger most handsomely when he delivered the official document—signed by King Philippe of France and sealed by *le Parlement de Paris*—to me personally. So that I could deliver it myself to my nephew, King Guillemin of Finistère. In time for Sir Bastien to compete in the

Yuletide Joust."

Gabrielle flew out of her chair and threw herself in Bastien's outstretched arms.

Swirling her into the air in a circular whirl, Bastien whooped with delight as he kissed her hair, setting her down at last upon unsteady legs, trembling at the incredible news.

King Guillemin raised his goblet of wine, prompting his guests to do the same. Hazel eyes twinkling with Yuletide joy, he proposed a triumphant toast. "To Bastien de Landuc, *le Marquis de Cornouaille*. May the Goddess grant you victory to win my daughter's hand. Become my royal son-in-law. And the future King of Finistère."

Chapter 13

Les Commençailles

The tangy brine of ocean spray crashing against the craggy cliff below *le Château de Beaufort* filled the cold December air as Ugolin strode across the tournament field under the overcast sky with his champion Sir Tréguier at his side. While grooms led the horses away toward the tents allocated for their lodging, the two men headed to the pavilion where enrollment was taking place for the Yuletide Joust.

Scattered across the tournament field, acrobats and performers practiced daring stunts while musicians and dancers rehearsed routines near the row of brightly colored silk tents established for the entertainers. Knights participating in tomorrow's opening ceremony, *les commençailles,* practiced weaponry with the swords, daggers, and battle axes to be used during the stunning preliminary performance.

Taking his position in line behind several other nobles who intended to compete for Princess Gabrielle's coveted hand in marriage, Ugolin was stunned to see Bastien de Landuc at the registration table where judges from Paris inspected the documents he had placed on the table before them. With a nod of approval, one of the judges wrote Bastien's name on the list of competitors while the other rolled up the document, tied it with black ribbon and handed it back to Bastien with a cordial, "Good luck in the tournament, *Monsieur le Marquis*."

Ugolin glowered at the dark-haired Master of Horse who returned his hateful stare with daggers in his eyes as he and his young squire exited the tent. How on the Goddess' green earth did Bastien de Landuc manage to register for the Yuletide Joust? Onfroi's men had ambushed and killed the royal messenger. They'd intercepted King Guillemin's *lettres patentes* before the proclamation ever reached *le Parlement de Paris*, delivering it instead to Ugolin. And he had burned the damned thing himself. Somehow, de Landuc had managed to procure a duplicate. A violent shudder of repressed rage rippled up Ugolin's scrawny spine.

Having arrived at the registration table, he handed his own documents authenticating his title of nobility and registered Sir Tréguier as the champion who would compete in the joust on his behalf. Once the enrollment process was complete, Ugolin and Tréguier exited the tent and remained with the other registrants as instructed. The sixteen nobles who would be competing in the Yuletide Joust waited outside the pavilion for the judges to finalize the registration process and inform the challengers of the rules for the tournament.

Bile rising in his raging throat, a corner of his lip upturned in a sneer, Ugolin glowered at Bastien de Landuc. whose fierce, predatory gaze fixed upon him in return.

The voice of the official from Paris rose above the clamor of the gathered crowd.

"The Yuletide Joust begins tomorrow morning at ten o'clock with the opening ceremony, *les commençailles.* An afternoon of theatrical and musical performances will follow, culminating in an evening celebratory feast. The following day, on the fifteenth of December, you sixteen nobles shall compete in the official tournament, consisting of three charges per course. Eight contestants will be defeated by the end of the first round. After an intermission, the competition will resume at noon, with two more challenges and elimination of contenders, resulting in two finalists for the concluding round. After a second intermission, the championship of the Yuletide Joust shall take place at approximately two o'clock. The victor shall receive five hundred gold coins, five magnificent warhorses, and Princess Gabrielle's hand in marriage, including her royal dowry—the Kingdom of Finistère."

Eager nobles exchanged greedy grins with the valiant knights who would represent them in the tournament. Of the sixteen contenders, only Bastien de Landuc, Thérouac of Dinan, Bergeron of Fougères and Audric of Sauterne had not selected a champion to joust on their behalf, preferring instead to rely on their own chivalrous skills and prowess.

The shrill, strident voice of the second judge rent the raucous din. "In accordance with *Le Statut des Armes,* all competitors in the Yuletide Joust shall abide by the rules of chivalry. Lances will be blunted and inspected prior to each run. Points shall be awarded for shattering the weapon against an opponent's shield or armor. Any challenger thrown from his horse will be immediately eliminated, and his rival granted the victory. Striking an opponent's horse or deliberately inflicting a grievous wound shall result in immediate elimination from the tournament. Chivalrous conduct and adherence to *Le Statut des Armes* will be strictly enforced, with violations resulting in disqualification. Good day, *messieurs.* Good luck to one and all."

As the competitors departed, Ugolin spoke to Tréguier as they crossed the tournament field and returned to the cluster of tents where the banners displaying the coat of arms of Nantes whipped in the winter wind. "You and de Landuc will be in the final round. You're by far the finest jousters in the group." They halted at the entrance to the group of pavilions where the knights that Ugolin had brought from *la Tour de Kerloch* practiced weaponry in preparation for *les commençailles.*

Or an attack on *le Château de Beaufort*.

Ugolin grinned wickedly as he watched the exceptionally skilled knights he had personally selected for this paramount mission. They would entertain the spectators in tomorrow's opening ceremony of the Yuletide Joust. And be prepared, if necessary, for Ugolin's command to attack. One way or another, he would claim Gabrielle's hand. *Le Château de Beaufort.* And the Kingdom of Finistère. Delicious chills rippled down his sinister spine.

A lithe female figure flew high into the air as acrobats rehearsed their performance near the long row of red silk pavilions. "Tomorrow, we observe *les commençailles* and enjoy the entertainment." Ugolin's body stirred as his lusty gaze followed the slender figure clad in sumptuous turquoise silk. *Perhaps I'll visit her tent tonight.*

His sensual reverie was brusquely interrupted by the sight of a groom leading Bastien de Landuc's stallion back to the lodging area. With a jut of his chin, Ugolin indicated the massive black warhorse. "That's de

Landuc's Percheron. Have your squire mix the yew needles into his feed the morning of the Yuletide Joust." His gaze followed the stable hand as he led the horse back to the group of white tents where the heraldry of *la Cornouaille*—the golden horned silver ram on the solid blue background—symbolized Bastien de Landuc's newly appointed title of Marquis of that region of Finistère. Ugolin glanced at Tréguier, whose gaze followed the groom and the destrier. "It takes about three hours for the symptoms to occur. Perfect timing for the final round of the joust. With his horse disoriented and skittish, you'll have no trouble unseating him." At the clash of swords and guttural grunts coming from his knights, Ugolin remarked with a snide grin, "And if, against all odds, Bastien de Landuc should somehow prevail in the Yuletide Joust—our men will already be in position, awaiting my order to attack. With the castle surrounded, King Guillemin will have no choice but to give me his daughter. And the kingdom of Finistère."

****

Gabrielle locked eyes with Bastien across the dinner table where he sat with his two brothers Gaultier and Cardin as servants cleared away the dessert plates and refilled goblets of wine. Desire danced in the emerald eyes which sent scorching flames to every part of her quivering body. She longed to be alone with him but knew he would soon return to the tents and rejoin the knights preparing for the opening ceremony of the Yuletide Joust in the morning. The message was clear in his smoldering eyes. He longed for her, too.

Silver goblets sparkled in the candlelight from the crystal chandelier overhead as Gabrielle glanced around the rectangular table where her father sat across from her at the opposite end. To his left, her great aunt Béatrice and the three traveling companions from Paris-—Agnès, Clothilde, and Françoise, whom her father had felt obligated to invite to dinner—sat with Clothilde's husband Onfroi.

Le Vicomte de Vannes. Powerful ally of Ugolin le Clou. Whose men had ambushed and killed the royal messenger that her father had sent to Paris with Bastien's decree of nobility.

An ominous shiver rippled up Gabrielle's spine as Onfroi's sinister gaze fixed her with the stark stare of a predator.

"Dinner was delicious, Your Majesty. Thank you very much for your gracious hospitality. We shall retire now, to allow you sufficient rest." Viviane, seated beside her son Lancelot, smiled warmly at King Guillemin.

"You must remember to drink the ginger and tart cherry tonic for your gout, Papa." Gabrielle met her father's bemused gaze, remarking how much the color had improved in his gaunt, pale complexion. "I prepared it earlier, for Ezhvin to serve in your private chambers."

"I am certain he would not allow me to forget." The king chuckled as he glanced at the royal chamberlain waiting patiently with the other servants along the wall near the carved walnut sideboard. Directing his attention to Viviane, he added enthusiastically, "The treatments have helped tremendously. I am most grateful for your extensive knowledge and impressive skills."

The Lady of the Lake smiled discreetly, as did her son Lancelot, whose grin lit up his handsome face.

"You do have the rosy glow of health, Guillemin. I, too, am most grateful for your skilled healers and their diligent care." Béatrice bowed her silver-haired head in a nod of acknowledgement to the three priestesses sitting across the table from her.

King Guillemin's hazel eyes twinkled in the candlelight as he beheld Ghislaine, sitting alongside her husband Gaspard on Gabrielle's right. "The essential oils and foot massage have been simply divine. The inflammation and swelling have diminished considerably, and my appetite has returned." The king chuckled, gesturing to the crumbs of pastry remaining on the empty dessert plate as a servant whisked it away with a humble bow. "I look forward to a good night's sleep, free from pain. The first in a very long time."

"Since the royal physician Isnard began treating you, Papa." Gabrielle smiled gratefully at the three priestesses who had diagnosed her father's symptoms of nightshade poisoning. "Thank the Goddess, he is no longer here. And these gifted healers have restored your good health."

"Indeed. I feel like a new man." King Guillemin rose majestically to his feet, prompting Ezhvin and two valets to rush forward, eager to escort their royal sovereign to his private chambers.

The remainder of the guests rose to bow collectively before the retiring monarch.

"I bid you all a pleasant evening," the king said affably as he kissed Gabrielle and Béatrice goodnight, accepting Ezhvin's offer of a supportive elbow. "We'll see each other again tomorrow morning for the opening ceremony of *les commençailles.* Until then—*bonne nuit*. Goodnight, everyone."

Amid handshakes, hugs, and kisses of farewell, the king departed, and attendants arrived to usher his royal guests from the private solar.

Laudine and Ghislaine kissed their husbands, and Viviane said goodnight to Lancelot, for the men were returning to the tents on the tournament field where trusted knights stood guard over the horses and the exuberant boys Gaston, Quentin, and Max.

Bastien, Gaultier, and Cardin kissed their mother Laudine goodnight as the three priestesses exited the solar with attendants to escort them back to their guest rooms in the castle.

Gabrielle kissed Béatrice's cheeks in *la bise* of farewell as her great-aunt hugged her affectionately and whispered, "Goodnight, *chérie.*" A sweet smile crinkled her soft cheeks as Bastien gallantly kissed her hand. "Good luck, Sir Bastien de Landuc. My Yuletide wish is for you to win Gabrielle's hand. May the Goddess grant you victory, *Monsieur le Marquis de Cornouaille.*"

With a polite "*Bonne nuit,*" Gabrielle bid goodnight to her great-aunt's female traveling companions. And to Lord Onfroi, *le Vicomte de Vannes,* whose bleak stare and cold hands sent shivers of dread up her quivering arms.

In a rustling swish of mauve silk, Béatrice departed the royal solar with her Parisian entourage, escorted by the attendants who had accompanied them from *le Palais de la Cité*.

Once the vultures were gone, Gabrielle sighed in relief as she turned to bid farewell to Gaultier and Cardin, who approached with his intended bride, Charlotte.

"Tomorrow, during the opening ceremony, I'll defend Gabrielle and Charlotte in the stands, alongside Gaultier and a dozen royal guards who will protect the king and his honored guests." Cardin glanced at his oldest brother. "Prince Kaherdin and Princess Gargeolaine will be among the royal spectators, so we'll have the knights of Armorique for additional defense as well." He returned his attention to Bastien, a hearty grin stretching across his ruggedly handsome face. "We'll all be cheering for you during the joust." Cardin smiled gallantly at Gabrielle. "Will you be wearing your lady's colors?"

Bastien slid his arm around Gabrielle's waist and pulled her possessively to his side. "Indeed, I will. She'll tie an emerald silk ribbon on my lance for good luck." He kissed her hair, his ragged breath hot in her ear.

Gabrielle's' legs went weak as she swooned against him.

His deep green eyes ablaze, he lowered his face to chivalrously kiss her hand, his soft lips scalding her sensitive skin. "Granted with her favor… wearing her colors…how can I help but win my Lady's hand?" He flashed her a dashing, dazzling grin that took her breath away.

"May the Goddess grant you victory." Gaultier gripped Bastien's shoulder in a wish of good luck. With an elegant bow, he kissed Gabrielle's hand, bid them goodnight, and strode out of the solar.

Alone at last, Bastien whirled her into his arms and pulled her close, wrapping her in a snug embrace. "Mmmm," he hummed, sliding his silky tongue along the inside of her upper lip. "You taste *divine*." Pressing his hard body firmly against her stomach, he moaned, "I long for more…"

"So do I." Taking him by the hand, Gabrielle led him down the darkened hall where sweet smelling beeswax candles burned in sconces on the whitewashed stone walls. She opened the carved golden oak door leading into her royal chambers, and dismissed her servants with a toss of her head.

And welcomed Bastien into her rose-scented bed.

****

Ribbons of white clouds rippled in the pale December sky, the salty brine of the ocean breeze mingling with the tantalizing aroma of sizzling sausages and cinnamon pastries emanating from the red silk tents where merchants sold food for the hundreds of spectators gathering for the opening ceremony of the Yuletide Joust. Grooms led horses adorned in *caparisons* – elaborate cloth coverings emblazoned with the coat of arms of their riders-- lining the animals up in the lists as armored knights mounted their chargers for the preliminary round of jousting. Lively music of fiddles and flutes filled the festive air, as highest-ranking nobles flocked to the *berfrois*—the grandstand reserved for privileged guests to be seated near King Guillemin and Princess Gabrielle of Finistère. Swarms of jubilant, exuberant spectators lined up along one side of the tournament field, opposite the pavilions where brightly colored heraldic banners flapped in the winter wind and knights participating in *les commençailles*—the preliminary jousting events-- awaited their turn in the lists.

In the royal grandstand—defended on each end by Gaultier, Cardin, and a dozen knights of Finistère—Gabrielle sat between her father and Béatrice, who was flanked by her three Parisian companions and Lord Onfroi, *le Vicomte de Vannes*. On her father's left side, Prince Kaherdin and his wife Gargeolaine were protected by their royal guards from the neighboring kingdom of Armorique. Among the visiting nobles, Gabrielle spotted Ugolin le Clou and his father, Robert Cauchon, thankfully seated several rows to the right of Viviane, Laudine, Ghislaine, and Charlotte, who were nestled comfortably behind Gabrielle.

Ugolin's predatory stare fixed her like paralyzed prey as he stood to address her with a gallant bow. "Good day, Princess Gabrielle. How lovely you are in deepest green. Like a priceless emerald, sparkling in the morning sun." His upper lip curled into a greedy grin, revealing elongated, pointed yellow teeth. "I look forward to tomorrow's Yuletide Joust with unbridled anticipation. For my champion, Sir Tréguier, shall win me your coveted hand." His long tongue flickered across his thin, parched lips like a snake poised to strike. "I cannot wait for you to become my wedded wife." With a lascivious grin which made the hairs on the back of her neck rise in a frisson of dread, Ugolin swept his black velvet cloak with a majestic swirl and took his seat beside his smirking, gloating father.

Her mouth suddenly dry, her stomach clenched in a tight knot, Gabrielle's limbs shook as a violent shudder shivered up her spine. *I cannot marry Ugolin le Clou. Please, dear Goddess, may Bastien win the Yuletide Joust!*

A trumpet blast indicated the preliminary joust was about to begin. An expectant hush silenced the jubilant crowd who watched with bated breath as the red flag dropped, and two knights thundered down the grassy lists atop their destriers, lances aimed at each other's plated armor. Shrieks of excitement rent the crisp, salty air as the pointed coronel head of the winner's lance shattered against his opponents' shield.

Grooms led the next duo of jousting rivals to the starting position for their arms to be inspected, and soon, the flag dropped again, and another winner triumphed before the roaring crowd. By noon, the three different competitions of *les commençailles*—the joust, the sword, and the dagger—saw the top four winners in each event receive bags of gold and silver, with offers of sponsorship and patronage from high-ranking nobles for the knights who had displayed such impressive, chivalrous skills.

Musicians began playing, signifying the afternoon entertainment, as acrobats, dancers, and performers filled the castle grounds. Amidst lively melodies and squeals of delight, Gabrielle accepted the trencher of roast boar and honey, the cinnamon swirled pastry, and the goblet of fruity wine from attendants serving the royal guests in the grandstand. Savoring the delightful contrast of salty and sweet, Gabrielle deliberately avoided Ugolin's unrelenting, watchful gaze and concentrated instead on the daring acrobatic feats, dazzling array of bright silks, and lively, invigorating music emanating from the center of the castle grounds.

When they had finished eating, Charlotte—Cardin's betrothed—whispered in Gabrielle's ear. "I need to visit the garderobe. Would you like to come with me?"

Gabrielle nodded and rose to her feet, handing the empty trencher and wine goblet to an awaiting attendant. "I'll be back soon, Papa," she said, planting a soft kiss upon his bearded cheek. "Charlotte and I want to stretch our legs a bit." With a wave goodbye to Béatrice and the trio of healers who chatted gaily about the thrilling opening events, she and Charlotte climbed down the stairs to exit the grandstand, escorted by Cardin and six royal guards of Beaufort.

"I've noticed how Ugolin le Clou never takes his eyes off you. It's upsetting and unnerving. He is positively vile!" Charlotte linked her arm through Gabrielle's as they strode towards the designated tents. "I cannot wait for Bastien to trounce Sir Tréguier and win your hand. Then, once Cardin and I are married…" she exhaled breathlessly, flashing her grinning betrothed a dazzling smile, "…you and I will be sisters-in-law. *Family.*" Her blonde curls tousled by the crisp ocean breeze, her pink cheeks flushed by the cold bite of the Breton wind, Charlotte squeezed Gabrielle's hand affectionately as they entered separate tents to use the private chamber pots.

They returned to the grandstands to watch the theatrical performances, cheering and applauding along with the appreciative audience. Soon, privileged guests and competitors in the Yuletide Joust headed toward the castle for an evening feast and continued revelry while squires, grooms, and lesser knights remained near their pavilions to guard the horses and prepare more simple fare over open campfires.

Inside the expansive Great Hall, lively music of rebecs, flutes, and fiddles floated upon the tantalizing aromas of roasted meats and savory herbs wafting through the air. Crystal chandeliers suspended from the intricately beamed wooden ceiling sparkled over dozens of linen covered tables where goblets and silverware glittered in the incandescent light. Liveried valets ushered King Guillemin, Princess Gabrielle, and visiting sovereigns to the sumptuous royal table situated upon an elevated dais overlooking the Yuletide Feast. And, perpendicular to the royal stage, dozens of knights, ladies, and noble guests chatted amicably while castle servants placed platters of stuffed pheasant, roast boar, grilled venison, and baked trout amid heaping bowls of squash, turnips, peas, carrots, cabbage, and leeks.

Among the sixteen knights competing in the Yuletide Joust who were seated at the table of honor before the royal dais, Gabrielle spotted Bastien. Like the ephemeral wings of a tiny bird, her heart fluttered wildly as his deep green gaze bore into her very soul. *Please win my hand tomorrow. I cannot marry anyone but you.* She inhaled deeply, willing him to read the desperate message in her pleading eyes.

His dazzling smile seared her soul.

Throughout the evening, Gabrielle watched Bastien chat with his brothers, converse with other knights, and laugh with Lancelot and his father, Sir Esclados le Ros. His confident, relaxed demeanor reassured her, bolstering her courage to face tomorrow.

Where her future would be determined by the winner of the Yuletide Joust.

As the dessert dishes were being cleared, Sir Tréguier approached the royal table and dipped into a chivalrous bow. His dark hair gleaming in the candlelight, he rose to his full, impressive height and stood proudly, his brutally handsome face searching hers as his deep, resonant voice filled the cavernous hall. "Princess Gabrielle, I am Sir Étienne de Tréguier, champion of *le Vicomte de Nantes.*" He gestured gallantly across the room to the angular, ominous figure of Ugolin le Clou. "Lord Cauchon requests that you bestow your colors upon me for tomorrow's Yuletide Joust. Granting me your royal favor. That I may win for him your coveted hand in marriage." Sir Tréguier humbly bowed his noble head as he awaited her response.

Gabrielle darted a glance at Bastien. Jealousy flared in his feral, possessive gaze. As her eyes held his, she hoped he could read the message sent from her racing heart. *Only you, Bastien. No one else will wear my colors.*

Returning her attention to the dashing knight waiting patiently at her royal feet, Gabrielle replied regally, “I regret, Sir Tréguier, that I cannot bestow my favor upon you for tomorrow’s Yuletide Joust.” Her eyes locked on Bastien, whose rugged, scarred face blazed with savage longing. “For I grant my favor to *le Marquis de Cornouaille.”*

A hush fell across the Great Hall as Gabrielle rose to her feet, walked around the royal table to the edge of the dais, and beckoned Bastien to approach with a gesture of her slender hand.

Silence stretched across the room. All eyes fixed upon Bastien as he stood and strode briskly to stand before the royal dais.

Bristling with fury and indignant humiliation, Sir Tréguier was forced to step aside and cede his place before the Princess of Finstère.

“Sir Bastien de Landuc, present your sword.” Gabrielle’s melodic voice floated across the hushed chamber, clear as a clarion bell.

Bastien unsheathed his sword, laid it flat across his outstretched palms, and offered it to Gabrielle. His head bowed in humility, he lowered himself to kneel upon one knee.

Gabrielle unfastened the emerald silk ribbon from her long, cascading red tresses. Leaning carefully over the edge of the elevated dais, she gently placed the satiny sash upon the proffered blade. "I grant you my favor, Sir Bastien de Landuc. Wear my colors in tomorrow's Yuletide Joust. I wish you good luck, *Monsieur le Marquis de Cornouaille."*

With chivalrous panache, Bastien tied Gabrielle's ribbon to the hilt of his sword and sheathed it at his hip. "I am honored to wear your colors, my princess. May your royal favor grant me victory in tomorrow's Yuletide Joust."

Commotion carried through the Great Hall as Bastien returned to the table where Lancelot, Gaultier, Cardin, and Esclados clasped his shoulders with congratulatory cheers.

Heavy brows furrowed in a sullen scowl, Sir Tréguier lumbered across the room to the table where Ugolin le Clou and his knights glowered at Bastien in disgust and outrage. When the Black Knight seated himself among his fellow soldiers, Ugolin huddled with his champion and several soldiers from *la Tour de Kerloch*, as if conspiring against the fortunate contender who had won Princess Gabrielle's royal favor.

Upon the elevated wooden dais where Gabrielle sat with Béatrice and other visiting nobles, King Guillemin rose to his feet to address the assembled crowd. With a respectful nod to Prince Kaherdin and Princess Gargeolaine, the king announced, "Honored royal guests, distinguished nobles, and challengers competing in the upcoming tournament, I hope you have enjoyed today's opening ceremony of *les commençailles*, the splendid performances of theatrical and musical entertainment, and tonight's festive feast." Raising his chalice in tribute to propose a toast, his deep voice carried across the Great Hall with restored vim and vigor. “Let us drink to tomorrow’s Yuletide Joust. May each knight compete with chivalrous honor and prowess. And may the champion be worthy of my beautiful daughter’s hand in marriage. And the kingdom of Finistère.”

Goblets raised amid shouts of “Hear, hear” —royal guests, dignitaries, and knights alike all drank to the success of the Yuletide Joust.

Standing beside his throne upon the royal dais, King Guillemin bowed to dismiss the crowd and conclude the Yuletide Feast. “And now, *messieurs dames,* as we part company, I bid you a fond farewell. To the challengers in the Yuletide Joust, the best of luck to all. Until tomorrow. Goodnight, everyone.”

Attendants ushered royal sovereigns to private chambers within the castle and other noble guests and competing knights excited the Great Hall to return to their respective pavilions. Bastien—as Gabrielle’s personal royal guard—escorted her up the stone spiral stairs, down the candlelit corridor, to the golden oak door where she dismissed two dutiful knights.

And led Bastien in.

Locking the door behind them, she spun toward him, threw her arms around his neck, and pulled his impassioned face down to hers. She sucked his lips into her own and fervently kissed his bristled chin as he wrapped his arms behind her back and drew her body firmly against his. Gazing up into his fierce, feral eyes, she whispered breathlessly, “You’ve already won my heart, Bastien. But tomorrow, you must win my hand.”

He nuzzled her neck and raised a savage, haggard face. Desperation and desire blazed in his intense, anguished gaze.

She gently pushed the tousled dark hair away from his stubbled cheeks.

"Wearing your colors…bearing your favor…how could I not prevail?" His ravenous lips sought hers, his possessive tongue probing and claiming every soft, succumbing recess. Nimble fingers unlaced her bodice and slid the velvet down her shoulders. Panting, his breath ragged, his skilled mouth suckled a tingling nipple, sending warm pulsations and a throbbing ache deep inside her very core.

He quickly shed his armor, his sheathed sword clattering to the floor. Enveloping her with corded, muscled arms, he laid her upon the rose-scented bed. Worshipped every inch of her quivering body with his wicked, wonderful tongue. And filled her empty ache with the liquid essence of his soul.

****

Gaultier, the First Knight of *le Château de Beaufort*, stationed four royal guards outside King Guillemin's private chambers and headed down the dimly lit corridor to inspect the rest of the castle. As he strode toward the stone stairwell leading to the lower level, he was joined by his father, Sir Esclados le Ros, Lancelot, and Gaspard. The three men had just escorted Viviane, Laudine, and Ghislaine to their guest quarters and were now returning to the tents on the tournament field to rejoin their knights, horses, and the three young squires—Quentin, Gaston, and Max.

"I pray that Bastien prevails tomorrow," Gaultier said cautiously to his father as they strode down the hall. "But Ugolin's Black Knight is undefeated. He's half a head taller… at least forty pounds heavier." He met Lancelot's grim stare. "Tréguier wants to win at any cost.

And after tonight—when Gabrielle refused to grant him her favor and bestowed her colors instead on Bastien in front of the entire court…he'll want revenge for that public humiliation." Gaultier abruptly stopped walking and locked eyes with his distraught father. "I'm afraid Tréguier will kill him. Not just for Ugolin. But for his wounded pride."

Lancelot gripped Gaultier's shoulder, his deep voice echoing against the cold stone walls. "Bastien is the finest horseman I've ever trained. Incomparable in the saddle. Unerring with the lance. He'll win the joust." Warrior eyes blazing with conviction fixed him with a steadfast gaze. "He loves Gabrielle. He cannot bear losing her to another. Have faith in your brother. Bastien will triumph in the Yuletide Joust."

Gaultier nodded, exhaling heavily. "You're right. I must have faith."

Esclados wrapped a chain mail clad arm around his oldest son's neck, his white teeth gleaming against his coppery skin. "He'll win the joust. Save Gabrielle. And the entire kingdom of Finistère."

Despite his gnawing apprehension, Gaultier grinned, and the four knights continued their trek down the long, dark hall.

As they turned the corner, Gaultier spotted a trio of unfamiliar knights lurking in the shadows. He grasped his father's arm, halting their approach. In a barely audible voice, he announced warily: "Three soldiers up ahead. Just outside the door."

With the keen eye of a warrior, Lancelot scrutinized and assessed the soldiers. "They're waiting to ambush Bastien. He must be inside, with Gabrielle." A swift whisper of metal sang softly as Lancelot unsheathed his sword.

Following his lead, Gaultier, Esclados, and Gaspard bared their blades and prepared to engage. Gaultier's deep baritone bellowed down the hall. "*Sortez!* Get out! *Now*!"

The three nefarious knights disappeared into the dark.

"My father and I will stay here and wait for Bastien. You two go down to the field. Check on the boys and the horses. We'll join you later." Gaultier returned his sword to the scabbard strapped at his hip as his companions did the same.

Lancelot ducked his chin and descended the spiral steps with Gaspard at his side.

"We're lucky we found Tréguier's men before they got Bastien. They would have beaten him, perhaps captured him—so he couldn't compete tomorrow. Whatever their intent, it was evil." Esclados sheathed his sword and leaned against the wall with a heavy sigh. Pensive, his brow furrowed, he announced, "We'll take turns standing guard throughout the night. And tomorrow as well. We'll take no chances with Ugolin le Clou or his bloody Black Knight."

Gaultier met his father's fierce gaze and nodded gravely. He would protect his brother as valiantly as he defended his king.

A while later, Bastien slid quietly from Gabrielle's room, startled to find his older brother and father waiting outside the oak door. "Why are you here?" he asked cautiously, raising an inquisitive brow.

"Three of Tréguier's men were waiting to ambush you when you came out the door. Good thing we found them first." Esclados clasped his son's shoulder.

"C'mon, let's go back to the tents."

In the foyer on the ground floor, Gaultier assigned four knights to go upstairs and guard Gabrielle's door. Satisfied that the castle was secure, he accompanied his father and brother and returned to the lists.

In the morning, the Yuletide Joust would begin.

Chapter 14

The Yuletide Joust

Sea gulls squawked in the early morning sky, the aroma of sizzling meats wafting in the cold, salty air as Max, Quentin, and Gaston stuffed the final bites of sausage into their hungry mouths.

"Sir Bastien, may I bring Quentin and Gaston with me to tend to the horses in the royal stables? With their help, I'll finish my chores and be back sooner. You'll be here with Drach, so is it alright if they come with me?" Max brushed the crumbs from his lap as he stood, wiping his mouth with the sleeve of his woolen tunic.

Bastien sat upon a large stone near his tent, sharpening his sword to ease the restless tension in his adrenaline-drenched limbs. He paused and glanced up at his squire. "That's fine, Max. Be thorough, but be quick. I'll need you back here to feed and groom Drach. And prepare him for the first run."

With an exuberant grin, Max nodded and replied, "Thank you, my lord. We'll be back soon." Signaling his two young companions to join him, he ran off toward the castle stables to tend to King Guillemin's royal mounts.

Grooms scurried about with feed buckets for the horses as activity increased among the tents lining the tournament field. Squires fastened and adjusted gleaming armor for the lords they served, while others dressed horses in caparisons bearing the heraldry of their riders. Delicious scents emanated from the red silk pavilions where vendors prepared foods for the spectators to purchase before the joust began.

Gaultier emerged from the tent, stretching his arms overhead. A squire served him a platter of sausage, bread, and honey, with a hearty mug of ale. He sat down near Bastien to break his fast. "Too nervous to eat?" he asked, taking an enormous bite and wiping his mouth with the back of his hand.

"My stomach's in knots. I can't." Bastien spotted his father and Lancelot breaking their fast near the cooks' campfire. When they finished, the two men headed toward the end of the tournament field to the starting position where they would inspect all lances prior to each run. Bastien took a deep breath and exhaled forcefully, shaking his arms to relax his limbs and calm his ragged nerves.

Gaultier rose and rolled his neck, glancing at the cluster of tents where Ugolin le Clou and the Black Knight were preparing for the first tilt of the joust. "Good luck today, brother. May the Goddess grant you victory as you win Gabrielle's hand." With a hearty slap on the shoulder, Gaultier returned to the tent where his squire awaited to help him don the gleaming, polished armor that he would wear in the grandstand while defending the king.

Lively music floated on the crisp winter wind as spectators began filling the stands. At the sight of Gabrielle's flowing red tresses, Bastien's heart stood still. Her glorious smile seared his soul.

Today, he would wear her colors.

And, by the Goddess, win her hand.

While he stood mesmerized by the sight of his flame haired, fire hearted Valkyrie, Max, Quentin, and Gaston came sprinting across the castle grounds.

"Sir Bastien," Max gasped, bent over his knees, struggling for breath. "Enemy soldiers… on horseback… behind the castle. We saw them just now."

With a jerk of his head, Bastien summoned Gaultier to his side.

The First Knight of Beaufort, clad in full plate armor, sheathed his sword, and strode briskly toward his younger brother. "A problem?" he asked, taking in the boys' harried faces and heaving breaths.

"Mounted enemy knights. Lined up behind the castle." Bastien returned his attention to Max. "How many?"

"At least three dozen, my lord. Behind the castle. On the bailey. Inside the curtain wall." Max looked up at Gaultier, staunch loyalty blazing in his fierce, resolute gaze. "We saw them just now. Near the royal stables."

"You did well to alert us." Bastien rested his hand on Max's lanky shoulder. "I need you to prepare Drach now for the first run. Fill his feed bucket, give him fresh water. Put on his caparison. It's almost time for the joust to begin."

"Right away, my lord. C'mon boys. Let's take care of Drach." Max led Quentin and Gaston toward the tent where the black stallion nickered in greeting.

His brow furrowed in concentration, Gaultier stared pensively at the castle. Strategizing. "I'll send fifty additional archers through the tunnel." He turned to Bastien, his brother's warrior eyes ablaze. "Lancelot already has his men in position near the lake, and two dozen knights from Landuc are stationed near the open moor where you used to train with Gabrielle." He glanced up into the royal grandstand where the Prince and Princess of Armorique were taking their seats beside King Guillemin and Gabrielle. "Kaherdin has two dozen knights here on the tournament field, and we have four dozen of our own. If Ugolin tries to attack, we'll take him by surprise."

Gaultier's aggressive countenance shifted, encouragement and challenge gleaming in his fraternal eyes like the finely polished armor he wore with chivalrous pride. "You, my brother, must focus on winning the Yuletide Joust. Leave the rest to me." With a reassuring clasp on both shoulders and a hearty grin, Gaultier strode purposefully across the castle grounds to confer with his king.

The blue heraldic banner of his new fiefdom, *la Cornouaille*—with the golden horned silver ram—flapped in the briny breeze as Bastien entered his pavilion. Two squires jumped to attention and helped him don his plated armor for the Yuletide Joust. When he emerged, adjusting his armor, Bastien glimpsed two dark figures darting away from his horse's tent. *What on earth were they doing here?*

Warrior instincts on full alert, he scanned the area, his eyes landing on Drach's feed bucket near the opening of the pavilion.

The hairs rose on the back of his neck.

He picked up the bucket and sniffed, detecting a strong, resinous odor like pine. Sifting the oats through his fingers, he filtered out long, slender yew needles.

Fatal if ingested.

A jolt of rage bolted through him like white hot lightning. *The bastards tried to poison my horse!*

As Max exited the tent to fetch Drach's feed bucket, Bastien grabbed it, stormed over to the campfire, and dumped the contents into the flames. "Yew needles," he spat, shaking with rage as he glowered at the baffled groom. "*They tried to poison Drach.*"

Horror dawned in Max's bewildered gaze. "Bastards!" He pried the bucket from Bastien's steely grip. "I'll wash it out. And get fresh oats. I'll be right back, my lord." Max dashed across the bailey toward the well and returned a few minutes later, wiping the clean bucket with a drying cloth. He refilled it with fresh oats and fed it to the ravenous, grateful horse.

Bastien watched his Percheron crunch the oats while Quentin and Gaston fetched him fresh water to drink. Inside the tent, Max prepared the caparison hood Drach would wear for the joust, bearing the coat of arms of *la Cornouaille*. When the stallion was finished eating, the younger boys watered him, and Max brushed his coat.

Since Drach wasn't running until the last of the eight tilts in the preliminary round, Max and the boys walked him for a bit, as did other grooms from nearby tents with their lords' horses.

Bastien gazed into the grandstand where Gabrielle sat between her father and her great-aunt. He spotted his mother with Viviane and Ghislaine. Beside Béatrice, he glimpsed the trio of pasty-faced Parisian ladies and the conniving Onfroi—*le Vicomte de Vannes* whose men had ambushed and killed King Guillemin's messenger.

As if he sensed Bastien watching, Onfroi cast him a baleful stare that evolved into a sinister sneer.

Bastien glowered at the pompous prick, then directed his attention to the flame-haired beauty who, Goddess willing, would soon become his wife. When he caught her attention, he kissed the emerald hair ribbon she had given him last night during the feast, tucking it securely inside his armor. He fisted his heart in a chivalrous gesture of fealty.

And unending love.

She dazzled him with a blindingly beautiful smile.

A trumpet blare announced the beginning of the Yuletide Joust. Two opponents in plate armor, their horses adorned in colorful caparisons bearing their respective coat of arms, heads protected by *chanfron* shields, were led to the starting positions on opposite ends of the tournament field where Esclados and Lancelot examined the lances for compliance with *le Statut des Armes*.

With the weapons approved, an official dropped a red flag, and the two contestants charged at top speed, lances held close, ponderous hooves thundering up the grassy field. With a resounding clash of metal, one rider was thrown from his horse, and his adversary declared the victor.

Six more jousts ensued, with an equal number of contenders eliminated.

And now, in the final challenge of the preliminary round, it was Bastien's turn to tilt.

Under the cold, cloudy December sky, his surcoat and horse displaying the heraldic colors of *la Cornouaille*, Bastien rode out onto the tournament field where Lancelot inspected and approved his weapon. On the opposite end of the field, his opponent, Sir Thérouac of Dinan, sat astride his own charger, clad in the distinctive red and yellow of his own coat of arms, receiving Esclados' approval of his blunted lance.

When the flag dropped, Bastien flew toward his

opponent, his lance couched tightly against his torso. Leveraging his body with the high cantle back of his saddle, he shattered the star-shaped coronal tip of his lance against Sir Thérouac's shield, scoring one point.

Returning to the starting position, Max handed Bastien a new blunted lance which passed Lancelot's inspection. The red flag dropped, and again, Bastien shattered the tip of his weapon against his opponent's red and yellow shield.

The Parisian official moderating the Yuletide Joust declared Bastien de Landuc the winner of his challenge. Bastien advanced to the second round of competition.

With the preliminary round of jousting complete, the first intermission began.

Lively music from flutes and fiddles floated on the briny breeze. Acrobats soared in the sky and shrieks of glee filled the festive air. Tempting aromas of fresh bread, meat pies, exotic spices, and sweets mingled with laughter and gaiety under the pale winter sun.

Outside his tent, Bastien removed his blue-plumed helmet and wiped his sweaty brow. Despite the cold bite of the salty Breton breeze, his heavy plate armor had trapped and intensified the heat he'd expended in the joust.

A congratulatory grin stretching ear to ear, Max offered him a goblet of chilled ale and two aromatic meat pies, which Bastien devoured with relish. *At least I can eat now. The physical exertion of the joust burned off some of the adrenaline.*

When she rose to her feet among the royal spectators in the stadium, his gaze was instantly drawn to Gabrielle. Accompanied by Cardin and four royal guards, she descended the stairs, strolling arm-in-arm with Charlotte toward the row of red silk tents where food vendors sold sumptuous fare and spicy, delectable treats. Her long red tresses blowing in the salty ocean spray, she spotted him watching her.

And flashed him a brilliant, glorious smile.

His eyes held hers across the grassy field. *You shall be my wedded wife, Gabrielle. A Yuletide bride, just as you wished. Dear Goddess, please grant me victory today.*

The herald's trumpet signaled the beginning of the second round of jousting, and spectators rushed back to their seats to view the thrilling event.

Eight challengers charged in four consecutive tilts. Bastien triumphed easily by unseating his rival—Sir Bergeron of Fougères—in the first run.

At the conclusion of the second round of the Yuletide Joust, the number of contenders was reduced by half. The semifinal round saw the elimination of two more challengers, and the final match was reduced to two competitors.

Sir Étienne de Tréguier, the Black Knight champion of Ugolin le Clou.

And Sir Bastien de Landuc, *le Marquis de Cornouaille.*

During the second intermission, actors in vivid theatrical costumes performed a bawdy farce, eliciting raucous laughter and lurid cheers from the appreciative audience. Musicians entertained with lutes, dulcimers, rebecs and flutes, and dancers performed with bright silk ribbons as they whirled and twirled in the wintry wind.

Finally, the trumpet sounded to announce the final joust, and Max led Bastien—atop a caparison clad Drach—to the starting position for Lancelot to inspect his blunted lance.

Bastien eyed the solid mass of his formidable, hulking opponent. The magnificent plate armor, gleaming in the afternoon sun. The splendid black ostrich plume unfurling over his *heaume* and the *chanfron* headpiece of his enormous black destrier. Sir Étienne de Tréguier, the Black Knight of Nantes, was daunting indeed.

His heart hammered in his chest. Adrenaline surged in his veins, making his mouth parched and his limbs taut and shaky. Bastien pulled the lance close to his body, adjusting the vamplate protection over his gloved hand.

The red flag dropped.

His heart lurched, and he shot off the starting point like a perfectly released arrow from a tightly drawn bow. Gripping his thighs against Drach's powerful sides for balance and increased striking force, he prepared to propel Tréguier from the saddle.

And was stunned by the explosive impact of the Black Knight's lance, which shattered against his metal helmet, jarring him nearly senseless.

Stars blinded him. He shook his head to clear his vision as he returned to the starting position. His pulse pounded in his throat, and a wave of nausea rolled over him. His head throbbed painfully.

Inhaling deeply, he willed himself to focus. Tréguier had scored a point.

And had nearly unseated him.

He had to land a blow this time. And score a point to even the odds.

Gabrielle's face floated before his eyes. At the thought of losing her to Ugolin le Clou, possessive fury surged in his veins, and he focused his entire being on striking Tréguier's shield.

The flag dropped.

Bastien became one with his powerful horse, absorbing every drop of raw, equine strength, channeling it with violent force into the coronal tip of his long, pointed lance.

And shattered it soundly on Tréguier's shield with such impact that the Black Knight whipped backward in his saddle.

But did not fall.

Bastien returned to the starting position, and Max trotted over from the tent to hand him a new blunt tipped weapon. Lancelot inspected it, gave a nod of approval, and Bastien lined up for the third and final run.

This was it. He and Tréguier had each scored a point. This final tilt would determine who won Gabrielle's hand. *Goddess, please grant me victory.*

The final red flag dropped.

Thunderous hooves churned up the solid ground, clumps of black earth flying high into the air, as Drach pounded forward, gaining momentum and speed.

Stabilizing his solid core against the high cantle back of his saddle, gripping his powerful Percheron with the brute strength of his muscular thighs, Bastien bolstered his warrior body and braced himself for impact.

And squarely struck Tréguier's shining shield.

Without shattering the star-shaped coronal tip of his accurate, unerring lance.

Both competitors returned to their starting positions while the two governing officials from Paris conferred. A point was scored by shattering the lance against an opponent's shield or armor, which each contender had done. Yet, if a lance did not shatter, but the rival shield had indeed been struck, would that result in a point being scored?

And therefore… victory for Bastien?

His heart hammered. Way too fast. Every muscle shook from the sudden surge of adrenaline. The pounding in his head from Tréguier's earlier blow sent another wave of dizzying nausea as bile rose in Bastien's rasping throat.

One of the judges strode into the center of the tournament field. With a collective intake of breath, an expectant hush settled over the exuberant, enthralled crowd.

"Each competitor has scored one point," he announced with an authoritative shout. "But no lance was shattered in the final run." The biting winter wind whipped his long black velvet cloak. "Therefore, the championship of the Yuletide Joust shall be determined by a battle of swords!"

Cheers rippled through the excited crowd, the commotion stilled by the official's raised hand. Inhaling deeply, summoning the vocal strength for the official proclamation, he cried triumphantly, "The first contender to disarm or overpower his opponent shall be declared the victor. May the best swordsman win!"

Amid hearty shouts and enthusiastic applause, both contenders dismounted.

Tréguier handed his reins to a groom who led the massive, ornately clad destrier back to Ugolin le Clou's cluster of tents. The Black Knight's squires dashed onto the tournament field and helped their lord remove the elaborate, ostrich-plumed headpiece and heavy plated armor which would hinder his vision and restrict his movement in the battle against Bastien. The Black Knight donned chain mail and leather armor instead, the cowl headpiece protecting the bridge of his nose without impairing his breathing. With chivalrous panache, he strapped on a studded scabbard and sheathed his impressive sword. In its elaborately carved hilt, a large black gem glittered in the slanting rays of the afternoon sun like the watchful, predatory eye of a giant serpent—poised and ready to strike.

Max trotted across the field and led Drach back to the pavilions where the blue banners of *la Cornouaille* flapped in the Breton breeze.

Lancelot and Esclados—no longer needed to inspect the horses and lances for the completed runs of the joust—jogged over to Bastien on the grassy plain amidst clumps of mud and imprints of hooves scattered across the castle grounds.

Like Tréguier, Bastien removed his plumed *heaume*, shaking the splatters of sweat from his dark, damp hair as his father helped him remove the heavy, plated jousting armor.

Gabrielle's green silk ribbon floated to the ground.

Bastien peeled off his glove and snatched it up with a bare hand, tucking it safely inside the soaked chemise which clung to his perspiration-laden body. *She blessed me with her royal favor. I must wear My Lady's colors.*

Lancelot smiled knowingly as he eased Bastien into the more flexible chain mail and leather which would allow him greater flexibility and agility. Battle fury blazed in his intense, savage gaze. "He's taller. Heavier. More experienced. *But slower.*" Challenge and conviction warred in his warrior eyes. "Use it to your advantage."

Resolute, Bastien held his former mentor's steadfast gaze, accepting both the sage stratagem and the proffered sword. As Lancelot and Esclados returned to the tents to observe the outcome of the Yuletide Joust, Bastien strapped his sheathed blade to his hip.

And, heart hammering, muscles tense as a tautly drawn bow, strode onto the field.

To challenge the infallible Black Knight.

****

Gabrielle couldn't breathe.

Bastien had just walked out onto the tournament field to battle Ugolin le Clou's champion. A surly, hulking brute several inches taller and about fifty pounds heavier than the valiant knight she loved with all her fiery Viking heart.

She gripped the sides of her green velvet gown, fervently whispering her Yuletide wish, willing with all her might for him to win.

"He's unparalleled with the sword, *chérie.* Bastien fought off four knights to defend you." Imbued with royal wisdom, her father's deep voice wrapped her in a warm, reassuring cloak. Hazel eyes twinkling in the golden sun, he said softly, "That's why I appointed him your personal royal guard." He squeezed her hand, raised it to the warm lips smiling above his silver-streaked beard, and bestowed a loving, reaffirming, paternal kiss.

The jarring clash of metal reverberated through her very bones.

Tréguier's relentless sword crashed repeatedly against Bastien's wooden shield like the thunderous waves pummeling the craggy cliff below the castle, the staggering impact causing him to stumble under the merciless, incessant assault.

Why does he not strike back? Why does he endure the brunt of Tréguier's blows without a reverse attack? Gabrielle's pulse pounded in her constricted throat, her breath shallow and fast.

The Black Knight lunged, heaving his heavy sword into a crushing, battering blow.

Yet Bastien deftly dodged the strike, whirling nimbly away as Tréguier toppled to one knee, thrown forward by the impetus of his own thwarted attack.

Clearly winded, gasping for breath, Tréguier struggled, attempting to regain his footing in time to meet Bastien's swift strike.

From his stance behind the exhausted, unsteady Black Knight, Bastien swirled in a deadly spin, smashing the full force of his weapon into a brutal, bludgeoning blow that toppled Tréguier to the ground. Seizing the enemy sword from the Black Knight's slackened grip, Bastien pointed the lethal tip of his own victorious blade against Tréguier's exposed throat.

The frenzied crowd erupted in raucous, riotous cheers.

Gabrielle shot to her feet, shrieking and jumping with joy. Tears streamed down her smiling face as she applauded wildly, her trembling knees weak with relief.

Béatrice hugged her tight, murmuring congratulatory praise as she kissed both her dampened, grinning cheeks.

Balancing his weight on his good foot, Gabrielle's father crushed her in a regal bear hug, then turned to face the jubilant throng. As he raised his arms over his crowned head, the ermine trim of his blue velvet cloak parted with magnificent royal splendor.

Bastien sheathed his triumphant blade and dashed

from the tournament field to stand before the royal grandstand where King Guillemin silenced the exuberant crowd.

"Sir Bastien de Landuc, as champion of the Yuletide Joust, I hereby grant you my daughter Gabrielle's hand in marriage. And bestow upon you her royal dowry. The kingdom of Finistère!"

Amid spectators' riotous cheers, shrieking shouts and frenzied applause, musicians began playing a triumphant refrain.

Gabrielle dashed down the stairs and threw herself into Bastien's outstretched arms, squealing with glee as he spun her in a circle, lifting her high in the air.

He placed her back on the ground and wrapped his chain mail clad, chiseled arms around her waist. Pulling her against his heaving chest, he claimed her lips with his own. "*Mine.* You're all mine. My beautiful bride."

An eerie, ominous horn blared, like the piercing howl of a monstrous, predatory beast.

Atop his warhorse, Ugolin le Clou clutched a cone-shaped, intricately carved ivory *oliphant* horn as he and a bevy of armored knights rode audaciously into the center of the tournament field. Summoned by their lord's bellowing blow, dozens of soldiers surrounded the royal grandstand, the tented pavilions, and the perimeter of the castle. Archers with nocked arrows targeted the king.

As Bastien stepped protectively in front of Gabrielle and unsheathed his sword, Ugolin le Clou halted his destrier in front of a panting, puffing Sir Tréguier. With a derisive sneer, he roared, "*You failed*!"

And beheaded the beleaguered Black Knight.

Amid gasps of shock and shrieks of fear from the petrified, stunned crowd, Gabrielle cast a calculating gaze over Ugolin's mounted, armored knights.

Viking warrior and Valkyrie, she astutely assessed the enemy.

She knew that Gaultier had positioned the castle archers behind the château near the lake. Lancelot had stationed his men in the dense woods to the north, and Esclados had placed his knights from Landuc near the moor where she had always trained with Bastien.

"King Guillemin," Ugolin shouted from the field atop his warhorse beside the bloodied, butchered corpse of his horrifically humiliated champion. "Your castle is surrounded." With a swooping, panoramic gesture, he indicated the multitude of armored knights that awaited his command. "The choice is yours. One way or another, I shall have your daughter. And her royal dowry. The kingdom of Finistère."

Gabrielle glanced back at her father, standing proudly among his royal guests. Loving, paternal eyes met hers as his noble face crumpled in despair.

"I'm an impatient man, King Guillemin." Ugolin leaned forward in his saddle, his gaunt face a grotesque mask of greed. "The Yuletide Wedding was scheduled for tomorrow. But I insist on marrying the princess today. At once. Either peacefully…. *or by force*."

Metal sang as Ugolin's knights swiftly unsheathed their swords.

Shrieks of terror shot from the crowd. Spectators on the sidelines dove into their tents. Frantic nobles in the grandstand tried to shield themselves behind Gaultier, Cardin, and King Guillemin's royal guards.

Gabrielle quickly weighed the odds.

Prince Kaherdin had brought at least two dozen armored knights. Lancelot's soldiers from *la Joyeuse*

Garde lurked among the jousting contestants near the competitors' tents. Gaultier, Cardin, and at least a dozen guards defended her father and his royal guests. And, among the thirty contenders of the Yuletide Joust and the numerous participants in *les commençailles*, not one favored Ugolin le Clou.

A brilliant plan dawned in her valiant Valkyrie mind.

"Follow my lead," she whispered in Bastien's ear. "Trust me. I have an idea."

Stepping out from behind a protective Bastien, Gabrielle strode a few feet toward her armed assailant, deliberately averting her eyes from Sir Tréguier's decapitated corpse sprawled ignominiously amid gruesome gore.

Ugolin le Clou sat his magnificent horse, eyeing her with malevolence, mistrust, and malice.

"Ugolin Cauchon, I wish to avoid bloodshed at all costs." Her clear, regal voice carried on the winter wind. "As the future Queen of Finistère, my primary concern is the sanctity of my people." Despite the quivering of her limbs and the twitching of her clenched stomach, Gabrielle stood tall, shoulders back, head high.

And mustered every bit of her ancestral Viking valor.

"I shall concede to your demands and agree to marry you. But I ask that you first grant me one royal request." Long red tresses whipped her cheeks, stinging in the salty spray.

Ugolin scanned the perimeter like a hawk sensing its prey. Seemingly satisfied with his superior strength, he grinned snidely at Gabrielle. "My beautiful bride, I wish to please you. What is your royal request?"

"I wish for you to allow the frightened spectators to depart at once from this tournament field. Please honor your future queen by ensuring the safety of her beloved people." Under her emerald gown, Gabrielle shook as adrenaline raced in her warrior veins.

He considered her plea, glancing at the row of tents where mounted knights awaited his command. With a reluctant nod of consent, he barked, "The knights and competitors remain here. Under my watchful guards. But the frightened spectators and visiting nobles…yes, my queen. Your future husband—and king—grants your royal request."

Black cloak flapping like the wings of a giant bat, Ugolin rode toward the grandstand to address the cowering audience. "*Messieurs dames,*" he drawled, the side of his hideous face curling up in a snickering sneer, "your future queen has a most generous heart." He shot Gabrielle a lewd, lascivious grin. "And I, your future king, have granted her request. You may leave at once, and I shall ensure the safety of your royal carriages. And your hastened departure."

Amid anxious gasps and muffled shrieks, frantic spectators—including the *Vicomte de Vannes* and the vicious vultures from Paris—poured out of the stands and scurried across the castle grounds like frightened mice evading a swarm of swooping hawks. Pavilions fell, whisked off the tournament field, as guests filed into their horse-drawn carriages and swiftly swept away. Musicians and performers, their theatrical costumes and instruments safely secured, fled for their lives in boldly painted, vividly colored, wooden caravans.

Within minutes, the spectators were gone. Gabrielle sighed in relief. And stepped toward the man she loathed.

Ugolin dismounted, tossing his horse's reins to one of his grooms. Cloaked in arrogance, gloating with victory, he strode confidently toward Gabrielle with an outstretched, gloved hand. "Come, my queen. To the white wedding pavilion. The Bishop of Nantes is waiting to perform the ceremony." He grabbed her hand and wrenched her against his scrawny body. Yanking her hair, he pulled back her head and placed the sharp tip of his dagger against her exposed throat. He licked the side of her face and panted in her ear. "I can't take any chances, my love. You will be mine. *Or you'll die*."

He shouted to Bastien, who stood paralyzed, his anguished gaze fixed on Gabrielle. "Drop your weapon, or I'll slice her pretty throat." A putrid tongue slithered over her pounding pulse like a venomous snake poised to strike.

With a jut of his sparsely bearded chin, Ugolin summoned two armed guards. "Take his weapon. And bring him here. I want him to watch as I wed…" he snickered lewdly, thrusting his hardened body against Gabrielle's' backside, "…and bed…his intended bride."

Trapping their prisoner between drawn swords, the duo of knights forced Bastien to surrender his blade. As they forced their captive to Ugolin's side, Gabrielle held Bastien's wretched gaze, messaging him with imploring eyes. *You trained me well. I'm a warrior. And I plan to fight.*

Comprehension dawned on his sullen, despairing face. The fury which blazed in his impassioned gaze told her that he'd understood.

And would fight to the death for her.

"Guard the king. And his knights. Keep them in the stands until after the wedding. *I want no interference*."

Ugolin jerked his head, and a bevy of soldiers galloped across the field, dismounted, and—swords drawn—positioned themselves at each end of the stairs leading into the grandstand.

Heart racing, limbs quivering, mouth dry, Gabrielle glanced up at the stadium where the remaining royal guests huddled together in fear.

Her father stood transfixed beside her great-aunt Béatrice and Cardin's betrothed, Charlotte. Prince Kaherdin and Princess Gargeolaine, defended by four valiant knights of Armorique, surrounded the trio of female healers who had cured the king. Gaultier and Cardin—Bastien's two brothers and her father's loyal, royal guards—stood protectively with a dozen knights of Beaufort in front of their sovereign monarch and his cherished royal guests.

Please, dear Goddess, help me save them. The man I love. And my beloved kingdom.

"I cannot wait to bed you, my beautiful Breton bride. As soon as the ceremony is complete, we're going into the castle to consummate our marriage." Ugolin grinned wickedly at Bastien. "And, before you are tortured to death… *you'll be forced to watch.*" The dagger tip pressing at her throat, Ugolin wrapped an arm around Gabrielle's waist, pinning her hips in place as he rubbed the hardened length of his body into her backside. He moaned into her ear. "Ugolin le Clou. *Hard as a fucking nail.*"

Between the pair of enemy blades, Bastien bellowed, "You bastard! I'll kill you!"

Ugolin cackled like a carrion crow.

Revolted, Gabrielle swallowed the bile rising in her throat, shuddering at the thought of his vile, repulsive body penetrating hers. Shivers rippled through her.

She gauged his strength and agility. Although he now had her in a compromising position with the dagger at her neck, he did not possess the honed body of a well-trained warrior.

But Gabrielle certainly did.

Ugolin le Clou liked to dominate women, whom he considered weak. He would be unprepared for a female who could fight. And Gabrielle would use this to her advantage now.

While he dragged her toward the white silk pavilion where the wedding would take place, Gabrielle pretended to trip on the hem of her gown.

Ugolin stumbled, as intended, loosening his hold on the dagger at her neck.

Just as Bastien had taught her, Gabrielle stomped on Ugolin's foot and rammed her elbows into his ribs. As her captor dropped the dagger and bent over in incapacitating pain, she wrenched out of his grip and swirled, sweeping her leg to dislodge the nearby supporting pillar.

Voluminous waves of white and heavy wooden poles crashed down, wrapping and trapping them in an enormous silk web. Gabrielle grabbed the dagger that Ugolin had dropped and slashed her way out, thrilled to see Bastien slay one of his two captors with a seized sword. Nearby, the other slaughtered knight lay motionless on the grass, blood pooling from a hideous gash at the base of his ravaged neck.

Spotting her emerging from the collapsed pavilion, Bastien's face shone with relief as he retrieved his surrendered sword from the fallen knight. Sheathing his blade, he grabbed the other enemy weapon and rushed to

Gabrielle's aid, handing her the stolen steel and shield just as Ugolin le Clou and four knights emerged from the rubble.

Gabrielle lowered herself into a crouched position and unsheathed her sword. Bastien, at her side, raised his *bouclier* shield and bared his lethal blade.

The booming bellow of Ugolin's ivory *oliphant* blasted through the air.

Like a horde of hungry locusts swarming tender stalks of wheat, armored knights on warhorses descended en masse upon the castle grounds. The clash of metal and shrieks of agony rent the wintry sky as Gabrielle and Bastien engaged the advancing enemy.

Atop destriers galloping from the jousting tents, Lancelot's knights from *la Joyeuse Garde* and Kaherdin's soldiers of Armorique joined the frenzied foray. Bastien's father, Esclados le Ros—the Red Knight of Landuc—stormed the battlefield with his troop of armored men. Dozens of King Guillemin's knights poured from *le Château de Beaufort*. And, in the distance, behind the castle, throngs of skilled soldiers squelched Ugolin's invading army with a swift, staggering, surprise rear attack.

As she slashed and sliced with her stolen sword, Gabrielle spotted Ugolin le Clou, his desperate gaze frantically scanning the tournament field where arrows from castle archers rained death upon his besieged men. He sprinted toward a saddled horse, abandoning his beleaguered knights.

The coward is trying to flee the battlefield!

Before Ugolin le Clou could escape, Bastien removed the villain's vile head with a savage slice of his sword.

Within minutes, bloodied enemy bodies littered the gruesome castle grounds.

Gabrielle glimpsed Lancelot and three of his loyal knights shielding Gaston, Quentin, and Max in one of Bastien's tournament tents. He flashed her a reassuring grin of relief, as Esclados and Jeffroi—second in command of the knights of Beaufort—rode triumphantly across the battlefield to report to the king.

Bastien wiped Ugolin's blood on the slain enemy's tunic and dashed to Gabrielle's side. "Thank the Goddess, you broke free of his hold." Sheathing his sword, he wrapped an arm around her neck as she dropped her own bloodied blade. He pulled her into his arms, kissed her hair, and whispered into her ear, "It's over. He's gone. Ugolin le Clou can never harm you again." Warm, fierce lips possessively claimed hers. "You're finally *mine*."

Sweat-drenched hair clinging to the sides of his ragged, haggard face, desperately clutching a shaking Gabrielle in his protective embrace, Bastien raised his head at the sound of approaching horses' hooves.

Dozens of their own victorious knights returned on horseback to the devastated tournament field, lining up around the perimeter to await orders. Three commanders rode to the grandstand where Gaultier, Cardin, and the royal guards of Beaufort protected King Guillemin and his overwrought royal guests.

Taking her hand, Bastien led Gabrielle across the bloodied field to stand before her father.

Sir Jeffroi, atop his Friesian warhorse, removed his armored helmet and bowed his head humbly before the king. Eyes gleaming with battle fury, he bellowed triumphantly, "The castle is secure, my king. Ugolin le

Clou is defeated. His army, eliminated."

Sir Rodolphe, one of the three commanders reporting to King Guillemin, shouted proudly, "Six pirate ships were spotted in our harbor. Catapults sunk three enemy vessels. Archers with flaming arrows destroyed two others. The final ship fled in terror. My king, I am pleased to report that our coastal waters are once again secure."

King Guillemin nodded in approval and recognition. "Ugolin le Clou coordinated an attack with his ally, the pirate Balthazar. You are to be commended for your valor and prompt response, Sir Rodolphe. You have honorably defended *le Château de Beaufort*, and I am indeed grateful for your heroic actions. You shall be well compensated." The king addressed Sir Thibault, his third in command. "Send scouts to patrol the castle grounds. Ensure that none of Ugolin's men remain lurking in the forest."

"*Oui, Votre Majesté. À vos ordres*." Sir Thibault fisted his heart in fealty, reined in his warhorse, and departed with a battalion of knights.

"Gather the bodies of our fallen soldiers. Prepare them for an honorable burial tomorrow morning. Burn the corpses of the enemy. Including Ugolin le Clou." The king issued orders to Sir Jeffroi, who departed immediately with his men to execute the royal command.

Young Gaston seated in the saddle before him, Lancelot trotted up to Bastien on his Percheron stallion. Quentin and Max rode destriers at his side. "Ugolin's father, Robert Cauchon, departed with *le Vicomte de Vannes*. They left in the carriage with the Lady Béatrice's traveling companions from Paris."

"A coward, just like his son." Bastien spat on the

ground, eyeing Ugolin's corpse with contempt and disgust.

From the royal grandstand, King Guillemin boomed heartily. "You, Sir Bastien de Landuc, are the winner of the Yuletide Joust. I congratulate you on your victory. And proudly grant you my lovely daughter's hand in marriage." Triumphant pride shone on his grinning, bearded face. "Once again, you have saved my daughter's life. And, thanks to the training she received from you, she was able to defend herself against Ugolin le Clou. To fight like a Viking warrior queen and defend Finistère."

He raised outstretched arms toward Gabrielle and Bastien. "My daughter and her intended husband. I bequeath my kingdom to you as my official heirs."

While Bastien and Gabrielle beamed with delight, wrapped in each other's arms, the king surveyed the destruction and devastation of the bloody battlefield before them. With a sad smile, he gestured to the trampled remains of the white silk tent. "Alas, *chérie,* my Yuletide wish to see you married this holiday season has been dashed as surely as that ruined pavilion. We cannot have a wedding here. "

Viviane's lyrical voice rang out like the peals of a bell. "King Guillemin, I would be honored to host the winter solstice wedding at my Crystal Castle."

All heads turned to the lovely Lady of the Lake.

"I've already planned to welcome guests for the holidays, Your Majesty. I have more than ample provisions. A skilled chef who is also a magnificent *pâtissière."* Viviane's irresistible smile was as convincing as her persuasive words. "The entire *château* is elaborately decorated for Christmas. I would be delighted to host the wedding and have you all as my royal guests for the entire holiday season. From the winter solstice wedding, throughout the twelve days of Christmas, including Twelfth Night—*la Fëte des Rois*."

Gabrielle tore herself from Bastien's arms and rushed to the bottom of the grandstand. Clasping her hands together as if in prayer, she implored her father with beseeching eyes. "Oh, please, Papa. Say yes! A winter solstice wedding in the Crystal Castle…it's my Yuletide wish come true!"

The king chuckled merrily. "*Ma fille,* when have I ever been able to deny you your heart's desire?" He flashed a magnanimous grin at Lancelot's mother. "Lady Viviane, we gratefully accept your gracious invitation. My daughter, royal guests, and I shall celebrate the winter solstice wedding of Princess Gabrielle and Bastien de Landuc, *le Marquis de Cornouaille*, at your lovely Crystal Castle. A perfect outcome for the Yuletide Joust, and a joyous holiday season for all." With an expansive gesture, the king added, "And now, let us go into the castle, to my private solar. We'll toast to the royal wedding of Gabrielle and Bastien. And celebrate today's victory with tonight's Yuletide Feast!"

The afternoon sun was setting over the turbulent sea. A crisp salty breeze floated through gossamer drapes of the partially opened window overlooking the craggy cliff as guests settled around the table in King Guillemin's private parlor. Evergreen boughs decorated the mantle over the fireplace where the scent of pine and holly blended with the tempting aroma of cinnamon, citrus, and brandy as Ezhvin and two valets prepared mulled wine over the open hearth.

Once everyone had been served a goblet of the

delicious brew, King Guillemin raised his chalice to propose a toast. "Let us celebrate the upcoming Winter Solstice wedding of Princess Gabrielle and Sir Bastien de Landuc, *le Marquis de Cornouaille.* We wish you a lifetime of love and happiness. To the future King and Queen of Finistère!"

Amid cheers and tears, Gabrielle and Bastien drank to their future, their hands clasped together in joy. Gabrielle's heart soared as she beheld the lovelight shining in Bastien's fierce Breton gaze.

As Gaston, Quentin, and Max sipped their goblets of mulled wine, delighted to partake of the same beverage as the adults, Lancelot chuckled and turned to speak to his mother. "Tomorrow, after the service for the fallen soldiers, I plan to ride home to *la Joyeuse Garde* with my knights and return the horses to my stables." He flashed a charming smile at Ghislaine and Laudine, seated with their husbands beside Viviane. "Would it be alright if Gaston and Quentin rode with me? I could use the help with the horses, and I'd like to show Gaston my *château.*"

Ghislaine smiled lovingly at her young son, anxiously squirming at the edge of his seat. "Gaston would love that. Of course, he may go with you."

Bright blue eyes widened with delight, Gaston grinned from ear to ear at Quentin as Laudine granted her permission as well.

Lancelot shot Bastien an inquisitive look, his deep voice filled with mirth. "Could you spare Max for a couple days? He's come with you to my castle each summer for nearly ten years now. He knows everyone—he could introduce Gaston and Quentin to my stable hands. My knights. And my horses."

Bastien eyed Max, who waited with bated breath for his lord's approval. With a hearty slap on the lad's shoulder, Bastien agreed. "These three have become inseparable during the Yuletide Joust. I'm sure Max will enjoy showing the younger boys around *la Joyeuse Garde*. Yes, I give my consent."

While the boys grinned from ear to ear, King Guillemin took a gulp of mulled wine and sat back in his informal throne. "*Tante* Béatrice, you and your attendant must ride in the royal carriage with Ezhvin and me. We'll accompany Prince Kaherdin and Princess Gargeolaine's private coach. And travel alongside the Lady Viviane's carriage—transporting the trio of gifted healers." A grateful smile crinkled his bearded cheeks. Eyes twinkling with paternal pride, he chortled, "I know my adventurous daughter will prefer to ride her horse *Marivée* alongside her husband-to-be. We'll depart the day after tomorrow. And arrive at the Crystal Castle with plenty of time to prepare for the Winter Solstice wedding." He reached across the table and squeezed his smiling daughter's hand.

"And now, my guests, I'm sure you would like to rest after today's tumultuous events. Tonight, we celebrate Gabrielle and Bastien's upcoming wedding—and today's victory over Ugolin le Clou—with the Yuletide Feast. Lancelot, Esclados, Prince Kaherdin—please invite your knights to join us this evening in the Great Hall. Until then, everyone… I bid you all good day."

As the guests rose from the table and left the royal solar, King Guillemin said to Gabrielle and Bastien, "I'd like the two of you to remain here with me for a few moments. I have something to show you." He inclined his head to Ezhvin, who bowed at the waist and slipped from the room, returning a few minutes later with a small, intricately carved wooden box, which he placed on the table before the king.

"Twenty-five years ago, I married your beautiful mother, Mélisende." His eyes aglow with nostalgic love, Gabrielle's father took hold of her hand and kissed it softly as his gentle eyes held her gaze. "I know you don't remember her, for she died when you were just three years old. But she made me promise that on your wedding day, you would wear this." He opened the *écrin* and displayed a gold ring with a large, round, faceted emerald encircled by a halo of sparkling diamonds. "This was her wedding ring. And now, *chérie*... it is yours."

Awestruck, Gabrielle reverently took the ring out of the tiny box and placed it on the third finger of her left hand. In the slanted golden rays of the setting sun, the deep green emerald blazed with verdant fire in a corona of brilliant white ice. "It's breathtaking! Oh, Papa, I shall treasure it always." She gently removed the ring and placed it back in the small wooden box carved with roses. Tears filled her eyes as her heart filled with joy.

The king placed a black velvet pouch on the table in front of Bastien. "This is for you."

Bastien glanced at Gabrielle in stunned surprise. He opened the pouch and withdrew a gold band adorned with a large emerald centered between two smaller diamonds. "That ring was my wedding band when I married Gabrielle's mother. I'd like you to have it as you marry my beloved daughter."

Bastien tried to slide the ring on his finger, but the fit was too tight for his enormous warrior hand.

"The goldsmith will adjust it before we depart for

the Crystal Castle." King Guillemin motioned for the royal jeweler, who now stood beside Ezhvin near the marble topped walnut sideboard.

At the king's summons, the goldsmith measured Bastien's hand and announced with a humble bow, "With Your Majesty's permission, I shall take the ring now. I'll enlarge it and return the wedding band to Ezhvin tomorrow afternoon."

"Thank you, Archambault." King Guillemin nodded his approval.

Bastien placed the ring back in the black velvet pouch, pulled the drawstrings tight, and handed it to the jeweler, who bowed at the waist and backed out of the room.

"Well, you two certainly have much to celebrate. I shall retire now to my chambers for a soothing foot massage and the curative tart cherry tonic prescribed by my gifted healers. I'm eternally grateful for the relief of pain from my gout." King Guillemin allowed Ezhvin to help him rise to his feet. Placing a kiss on Gabrielle's smiling cheek, the king shook Bastien's hand and exited the sun-streaked splendor of the luminous royal solar.

Gabrielle opened the jewelry box again to admire the sparkling emerald gem. "I'll wear my mother's wedding ring." Tears of joy brimming in her grateful eyes, she beamed at Bastien. "My Yuletide wish has come true. I shall be a winter solstice bride. And marry the man I love."

She wrapped her arms around his neck, leaned forward, and planted her warm lips on his smiling ones. Closing the jewelry box and clutching it tightly, she rose to her feet and took Bastien's hand. "Come, my champion…" she whispered softly as she led him out of the solar. "Let's celebrate your triumph in the Yuletide Joust."

Grinning from ear to ear, Bastien followed Gabrielle down the quiet hall.

Through the golden oak door of her private chambers.

And into her luxurious, rose-scented bed.

Chapter 15

A Wondrous Winter Solstice

Two days later, after celebrating the royal betrothal of Princess Gabrielle to Sir Bastien de Landuc with a sumptuous Yuletide Feast, followed by the solemn memorial service and burial of the fallen knights who had sacrificed their lives to defend Finistère, King Guillemin and his royal entourage headed east across Bretagne to the Forest of Brocéliande.

To the *Château de Comper.*

The glorious Crystal Castle.

In the royal carriage protected by the intrepid knights of Finistère, Gabrielle's father rode with his chamberlain Ezhvin, his aunt Béatrice, and her lady-in-waiting, Marcelle. Prince Kaherdin and Princess Gargeolaine traveled in their own coach with an escort of royal knights of Armorique, and the third landau carried Viviane, Ghislaine, and Laudine—the trio of priestesses who had cured the king.

Bastien's father Esclados had departed the previous day, shortly after the memorial service. He and Gaspard, along with their knights, returned the Ardennes and Friesian horses used in the Yuletide Joust home to the magnificent stables of *le Château de Landuc.*

The cold, salty air whipped her long red hair and nipped her stinging cheeks as Gabrielle rode her beloved horse Marivée through the dense woods beside Bastien. *How exhilarating to ride through the forest again. And revel in the freedom to marry the man I love.* Her heart overflowing with gratitude and joy, Gabrielle inhaled the crisp evergreen scent of pine and beamed at Bastien.

In the midst of a clearing in the forest where four shimmering lakes converged in the distance, Gabrielle spotted a white limestone castle gleaming in the afternoon sun, its glistening walls glittering like thousands of faceted gemstones.

Le Château de Cristal.

The magnificent Crystal Castle.

"It's spectacular!" Gabrielle cried to Bastien as they dismounted and handed their horses' reins to awaiting grooms.

His handsome face alight with the same unbridled joy galloping in her jubilant heart, Bastien offered her a gallant elbow as he escorted his bride up the wide earthen path.

Garlands of deep green holly with bright red berries adorned the golden oak entrance door where a large evergreen wreath welcomed guests with holiday cheer. Inside the entry, a cluster of mistletoe——sacred plant to the Celtic ancestors of the Breton people—bestowed the protective blessing of the divine forest upon the Crystal Castle.

Amiable servants flocked to meet the royal *cortège* as the three horse-drawn coaches arrived in front of the *château.* Opening the carriage doors to welcome Viviane's guests, attendants escorted King Guillemin and his entourage into the pristine castle where tantalizing aromas emanated from the vast kitchen.

"*Bienvenue.* Welcome to my Crystal Castle."

Brilliant color from the stained-glass transom window above the entrance door reflected off the crystal chandelier in the central foyer where Viviane greeted her guests. "My servants will carry your bags and usher you to guest rooms so that you may rest and refresh after your voyage. Please join us in an hour for the delicious meal that Sophie has prepared. *À bientôt, mes amis.*"

Since she and Bastien were not yet married, Gabrielle was escorted to the room she would share with her great-aunt Béatrice on the second floor of the castle. Inside the large chamber, a comfortable canopied bed was centered against the creamy plastered wall opposite a large window overlooking the forest. In the corner of the vast room, a lace covered table flanked by two mauve velvet chairs stood near a stone fireplace. Evergreen boughs and garlands of holly adorned the mantle where a welcoming fire crackled in the beautifully decorated hearth.

As attendants unpacked their bags and stored their belongings inside an elegantly carved wooden armoire, Gabrielle peeked through the mauve velvet draperies to glimpse the shimmering *Lac de Diane* surrounded by dense woods. *The heart of the Forest of Brocéliande. Where I—as a winter solstice bride—will marry the man I love.*

A servant entered the room with a steaming pot of fragrant chamomile tea, interrupting Gabrielle's pleasant reverie. Crossing the room to join Béatrice at the corner table, she gratefully accepted the proffered mug and sat down to enjoy the *tisane*.

Gabrielle gazed into the kind, crinkled eyes of her beloved aunt. "I am eternally grateful that you sent the message to my father so that Bastien could compete in the joust." She reached across the table and squeezed Beatrice's gnarled hand. "Thanks to you, my Yuletide wish to marry the man I love will come true. *Merci du fond du coeur, Tatie.* Thank you, from the bottom of my heart."

Béatrice smiled affectionately, her soft cheeks crinkling like thin parchment paper. "I know how much the two of you adore each other. I am overjoyed that you will be a winter solstice bride. And that the valiant Bastien de Landuc—whom you have loved since you were just a girl—will be your wedded husband. The future King of Finistère." She sipped her tea pensively, then set the ceramic mug down upon the table. Rising to her feet, she strolled across the room and fetched something from her travel bag. Returning to her velvet chair, she placed a black velvet pouch on the table in front of Gabrielle. "This belonged to my sister Isabelle—your father's mother—who died when you were but a babe. She would have wanted you to have this." With an encouraging nod, Béatrice insisted gently, "Open it."

From inside the velvet sack, Gabrielle withdrew a heavy silver artifact. Suspended from a loop of braided black leather cord, a semicircular shaped pendant with intricate detailing hung in the center.

"It's a Viking symbol called a *lunula*, which means "little moon". It belonged to your ancestor Ylva, a Valkyrie shield maiden descended from Rollon, the first leader of Normandy. It has been passed from grandmother to granddaughter in our family since the tenth century, when the Vikings first settled in France. The leather cord has been replaced, of course, but the *lunula* is original."

Gabrielle cradled the precious heirloom, her long

fingers caressing the intricate details of the palm-sized silver pendant.

"It symbolizes the lunar cycle and female fertility of the Viking goddess Freya." Béatrice smiled nostalgically as she watched Gabrielle admire the craftsmanship. "My grandmother Ursa gave it to my sister on her wedding day. And your grandmother Isabelle intended to give it to you." Béatrice's expressive brown eyes glimmered with unshed tears. "Since my beloved sister is not here to bestow this heirloom upon you herself, I shall take her place as a doting grandmother and pass the *lunula* to you on your wedding day." With a gnarled finger, she indicated the braided loop centered at the top of the moon-shaped silver pendant. "Hang it on the wall over your bed. May the *lunula* of your ancestor Ylva and your grandmother Isabelle bestow the fertility of the Viking goddess Freya and bless you with many healthy children." Her bony knees creaked as she rose to her feet and kissed Gabrielle's cheek. "One day, in turn, may you bestow this *lunula* upon your own granddaughter in the Viking tradition of our family Valkyrie."

Gabrielle rose and wrapped her arms around her great-aunt's frail shoulders, fervently kissing her crinkled cheek. "Thank you, *Tatie.* From the bottom of my heart." She hugged the *lunula* to her chest, rocking it like the babes she hoped she would bear Bastien. "I will treasure it always."

Her heart overflowing with joy, Gabrielle tucked the *lunula* back into the protective pouch. *Tomorrow night, I'll hang this over our bed and share the Viking tradition with Bastien.* As she imagined the wedding night to come, warmth and wetness throbbed between her legs, a hollow ache in her lower abdomen. Her legs shaking with desire, Gabrielle lowered herself carefully to the tufted velvet chair and sat down with Béatrice to finish the *tisane.* Her fingers caressed the heirloom, symbol of her grandmother's love and Valkyrie heritage. *I hope that one day, I will have a granddaughter of my own to carry on our Viking legacy.*

Dinner that evening was a delicious *potage* of vegetable and venison stew, baked pike and trout from *le Lac de Diane*, and Sophie's scrumptious quince and honey pie. Later, in the adjacent ballroom where evergreen boughs and garlands of holly and ivy decorated the whitewashed walls, Viviane's guests danced to the lively holiday music of fiddles and flutes while moonlight shimmered on the rippled surface of the glistening lake.

The next day, Lancelot arrived with the three jubilant boys, eager to share stories of swift stallions and chivalrous knights. At the jolly dinner table, over Sophie's marvelous wild plum *tarte aux mirabelles,* Gaston exclaimed, his blue eyes bright with wondrous delight, "Sir Lancelot promised that one day, I'll have a Percheron stallion of my own—just like Gosse and Drach!" Amidst much laughter and love, Viviane danced with King Guillemin while Bastien swirled Gabrielle, Cardin twirled his betrothed Charlotte, and Prince Kaherdin whirled his wife Gargeolaine in the festive, gaily decorated Yuletide ballroom.

The winter solstice dawned crisp, clear, and cold. Clean evergreen notes of pine entwined with the holiday scents of citrus, cinnamon, and cloves as Gabrielle sat at Viviane's vanity table, watching her wedding preparations through the reflections of the mirror.

Laudine—who would soon become her mother-in-law—tucked fragrant white hellebore blossoms into the green garland headpiece of holly and ivy woven into Gabrielle's long, thick tresses. "Hellebore is called the Christmas Rose, for it blooms in the winter. Perfect for a winter solstice bride." Laudine's amber eyes glowed golden in the gilded morning light. "The white flowers look beautiful in contrast with your glorious red hair." She kissed Gabrielle's cheek and squeezed her shoulders affectionately.

Gabrielle smiled warmly at Laudine, her happy heart aglow. *I've never known a mother's love. But now I shall.* Reaching up to her shoulder, she rested her hand gently upon Laudine's.

"And the dark green holly complements your emerald velvet wedding gown." Ghislaine lovingly arranged the verdant lace along the curved neckline of Gabrielle's gathered bridal bodice.

"And your mother's emerald ring. You, my dear princess, are a breathtakingly beautiful winter solstice bride." In the mirror, Gabrielle glimpsed joyful tears in her great-aunt's glistening eyes as Béatrice lovingly kissed Gabrielle's smiling cheek.

"They're ready for us in the castle chapel." The long sleeves of her gown draped like the elegant wings of a white swan, her black hair streaked with shimmers of silver, Viviane hovered in the doorway, the trio of moonstone gems in her necklace sparkling in the morning sun.

She looks like a Christmas angel, Gabrielle mused, as the melodies of flutes, harps, and viols floated into the festive room.

Her heart aflutter like the wings of a white dove, Gabrielle rose from the vanity stool and—escorted by liveried valets—followed Laudine, Ghislaine, Béatrice and Viviane down the hall to the elaborately decorated doorway where her father waited at the entrance to the castle chapel.

Resplendent in a red velvet robe trimmed in white ermine fur, a golden crown adorned with gemstones atop his regal head, King Guillemin's hazel eyes shone with paternal pride and love as Gabrielle linked her arm through his elbow and entered the music-filled chapel where she would become Bastien's bride.

Sunlight streamed through the ogival stained glass windows, casting rays of brilliant color like a divine blessing as flautists and harpists played along one side of the semicircular apse. Bouquets of sweet-smelling hellebore blossoms mingled with the pine scent of evergreen garlands draped upon the wooden walls of the dais where *Frère Laurent*—a monk from the nearby monastery of *le Mont-Saint-Michel* who had come to perform the ceremony—stood behind a table topped with white linen and softly glowing beeswax candles. Along each side of the center aisle, elegantly attired guests stood in the wooden pews as Gabrielle walked down the aisle with her father to join a majestic Bastien.

An ermine fur trimmed black velvet cloak draped his broad shoulders. Over black velvet breeches and black deerskin boots topped with matching ermine fur, he wore a deep burgundy tunic belted and edged in gold. As they reached the wooden dais, her father placed Gabrielle's hand in Bastien's, then took his reserved seat among the royal guests in the first pew.

"Sir Bastien de Landuc, place this ring upon your bride's finger and declare your wedding vows." His brown hooded tunic belted at the waist, his tonsured head bowed in reverence, the rotund monk handed Bastien the wedding ring which had belonged to Gabrielle's mother Mélisende.

Emerald eyes ablaze like the gem he slipped onto the finger of her left hand, Bastien's deep voice reverberated into her very bones. "With this ring, I promise to honor, respect, and love you. And only you. Till death do us part."

Her knees trembling under her deep green velvet gown, Gabrielle accepted the ring from *Frère Laurent* as he directed her to place it upon Bastien's finger and proclaim her wedding vows. Raising her face to hold Bastien's intense, impassioned gaze, she said, loud and clear for all to hear as she placed the ring upon his calloused finger, "With this ring, I promise to honor, respect, and love you. And only you. Till death do us part."

"I now pronounce you husband and wife. Seal your wedding vows with a kiss." *Frère Laurent* smiled patiently as the couple complied.

King Guillemin rose from his seat to congratulate the newlyweds. His deep voice resonating with Yuletide joy, he proudly exclaimed with a jovial grin, "*Messieurs dames*, I present to you my daughter, the Princess Gabrielle. And her wedded husband, Sir Bastien de Landuc, *le Marquis de Cornouaille*. Future king and queen of Finistère."

Festive music filled the air as guests congratulated Gabrielle and Bastien, then followed the bride and groom to the festive Great Hall where feasting and dancing ensued, lasting well into the evening.

"Come, everyone, follow me to the forest. It's time to celebrate the winter solstice traditions of our Celtic

Breton heritage." Viviane donned her deep blue cloak, encouraging her guests to do the same. Following their hostess out of the *château*, they strode across the snow-dusted castle grounds to the edge of the forest where the glowing light of the nearly full moon reflected on the shimmering surface of *le Lac de Diane*.

Viviane stopped in front of a woven basket lined in red velvet and filled with shiny objects at the base of a large, full fir tree. ""Like our Breton ancestors, we'll decorate our winter solstice tree with celestial objects and small gift offerings to the Celtic gods and goddesses. Each person will add one ornament to our holiday tree." A welcoming smile stretched across her lovely face, she announced, "Newlyweds first."

While warmly dressed servants delivered mugs of *wassail* made from brandy, apples, oranges, and cloves to the guests gathered near the tree, Gabrielle led Bastien by the hand to the basket of Yuletide decorations at the base of the fir. Selecting a glittering star made of silver cloth embellished with tiny beads, she hung it on one of the branches as Bastien chose a moon-shaped ornament made from woven cloth of gold.

When everyone had finished and the basket was empty, Viviane led her jubilant, laughing guests back into the Crystal Castle where a Yule log burned in the crackling hearth. Attendants took heavy cloaks and capes, refilling mugs of *wassail* as festive holiday music filled the joyous air.

Whirling in Bastien's embrace as they danced *la carole*, Gabrielle remembered the unforgettable evening in the tavern where she had given herself freely to this man she loved to the very depths of her soul. His arms wrapped tightly around her small waist, she buried her nose in the dark hair at the base of his throat, reveling in his earthy scent and shivering with sensual delight. Soon, they would make love as husband and wife.

And she would hang the heirloom Viking *lunula* over their marriage bed. *Perhaps I will conceive Bastien's child tonight.* Warmth and desire throbbed between her quivering legs.

A while later, in Bastien's room where servants had moved her bags and belongings, Gabrielle luxuriated in the delight of being alone at last with her husband.

Bastien sat on the bed, removing his boots and watching her. Desire danced in his dark eyes.

She retrieved the *lunula* from the black velvet pouch and placed it in his hand, nudging his legs apart seductively with her hips as she nestled close.

One hand holding the Viking heirloom, the other stroking her backside through the soft velvet of her wedding gown, he eyed her with an intriguing blend of curiosity, love, and lust.

She ran her fingers through his thick, dark mane, pushing strands of wavy hair away from his face as she leaned down toward his upturned, bristled chin. It's called a *lunula,"* she whispered, tracing her tongue along the inside tip of his parted upper lip. "A Viking fertility symbol to bless our marriage bed." Withdrawing the pendant from his open palm, she wriggled out of the grip of his muscular thighs. On the wall behind the bed, she hung the *lunula* from the nail that Viviane's valet Jacques had hammered into the wall at Gabrielle's request. With a seductive smile, she sauntered back to the bed and resumed massaging Bastien's thick, shoulder-length locks.

He unlaced the back of her dress with nimble

fingers, tugging the velvet bodice down as he pulled her toward him, pinning her in place with powerful thighs. Tingling with anticipation, her bare breasts lingered before his rapt face, her nipples aching for his soft, skilled lips. He slid his hands up her back as he suckled a perfect pink peak, easing her down onto the bed to remove the rest of her gown.

He spread her legs wide to worship her with adoring eyes before tracing the soft curls and sensitive folds of flesh with long fingers and skilled, probing tongue.

Empty, throbbing, and aching, she watched with bated breath as he quickly shed his clothes. Her eyes rove over his sculpted muscles covered with dark hair, a trail leading down his rippled abdomen to the ardent arousal which made her swoon. He knelt over her, parted her thighs with strong knees, scooped her hips up. And filled her empty depths with his abundant seed.

Bodies sated, souls entwined, they slept together for the first time all through the night.

And when they woke, made love again. In the early morning light.

****

The day after the wedding, Prince Kaherdin and Princess Gargeolaine departed with their carriage and royal entourage, anxious to return to *le Château Rose* in Armorique to spend the holidays with Kaherdin's father, King Hoël, and their young son Karenteg.

Cardin, his betrothed Charlotte, and a dozen personal guards also bid a fond farewell as they rode west to spend the holidays with loved ones in her family's *château*, as planned.

On Christmas Eve—*la Veille de Noël*—Gabrielle sat between her husband and her father at Viviane's holiday table where Sophie the splendid cook regaled everyone with a sumptuous Yuletide *Réveillon* feast. Guests gorged on savory soup made from winter squash and ham, roast goose stuffed with chestnuts, late harvest vegetables, baked pike from the lake, and the traditional Yule log cake, *la bûche de Noël.*

When gifts were exchanged Christmas morning, Gaston was thrilled with his new wooden sword and shield with three heraldic red diagonal stripes.

His expressive blue eyes bright with Yuletide delight, Lancelot knelt beside Gaston and asked, "Do you know why your shield has these three red stripes, which are called *bandes de gueules?"*

"Because they're your coat of arms. And you're my hero." Gaston stated proudly, adulation gleaming in his adoring eyes.

Lancelot chuckled deeply from his belly, mussing Gaston's hair with a playful rub. "I'm flattered to be your hero. But there's another reason why your shield has my *écusson.*" He smiled at Ghislaine and Gaspard, seated with Viviane and King Guillemin near the cozy hearth. "I've already asked your parents, and they have granted permission for me to offer this Yuletide gift. I'd like to bring you with me—as my own personal squire—when I return to Camelot."

Gaston's eyes enlarged in astonishment and awe. His mouth agape, he spun his head incredulously toward his mother. "*C'est vrai, Maman*? I can go with Sir Lancelot? And become his squire?"

Bittersweet tears glimmered in Ghislaine's loving, maternal eyes. "Yes, my son. It is indeed true. Sir Lancelot has chosen you. An incredible Yuletide gift, for which we are all most grateful."

Gaston flew into his mother's arms with a squeal of unbridled joy. "*Merci, Maman*!" Lifting an exuberant, jubilant face, he ran to hug Gaspard and cried, "*Merci, Papa!"*, before returning triumphantly to Lancelot's side.

Tall and proud, his glossy dark hair tumbling past his broad shoulders, Lancelot smiled down at the beaming little boy. "You'll be a page at first, until you're fourteen, when you'll become my squire. We'll train together every day with King Arthur's magnificent knights. Each summer, we'll return to l*a Joyeuse Garde,* and I'll teach you to care for my horses, just like I did Sir Bastien. You might even become a Master of Horse, like him. We'll visit your parents. And my mother, here in the Crystal Castle. And—when you're twenty-one—you'll become a Knight of the Round Table. Just like me."

With his disarmingly charming boyish grin, Lancelot chortled, "Well, what say you, Gaston de Brocéliande? Do you accept my offer?"

Nodding enthusiastically and exuberantly, enormous blue eyes widened in delight, Gaston exclaimed excitedly, "Yes, my lord. I accept!"

"Excellent. Now hand me your new sword and lower yourself to one knee." Lancelot received the wooden weapon and waited for the little boy to kneel at his feet. "Place your right fist over your heart and repeat this oath of fealty. *I pledge my sword to you, my lord."*

Before Gabrielle, Bastien, King Guillemin, and a room full of Viviane's Yuletide guests, Gaston swore a sacred oath of fealty to Lancelot as his mentor and lord.

Like in a knighting ceremony, Lancelot touched the wooden sword to Gaston's right shoulder, then left, and proudly proclaimed, "Sir Gaston, I hereby dub thee my official page." Helping the beaming boy to his wobbly feet, Lancelot shot a grin at Quentin and Max, who had each received new swords as Yuletide gifts. "Let's go train with my knights, shall we?"

With whoops of glee, the trio of boys shot out the door.

"I think I'll join you. I could use some exercise after Sophie's sumptuous holiday fare. Care to join us, Gaspard?" Esclados rose to his feet, stretching his arms overhead.

"With pleasure," Gaston's father chuckled as he bestowed a farewell kiss on Ghislaine's cheek.

Bastien gestured to the intricate sword with a dazzling emerald in the pommel that he had just given Gabrielle as a Christmas present. "Let's ride out to the lake and train with your new blade. Like we used to, on the heathered moor near the cliff." He kissed her hand, a fiery challenge blazing in his fierce warrior eyes.

"Yes… Let's go!" Gabrielle jumped to her feet and turned toward Viviane and her guests. "Please excuse us. We'll return in a couple of hours." Strapping her new sword at her waist with a flourish, she donned her warm woolen cloak. And, hand-in-hand with her new husband, dashed off to fetch their horses.

****

Viviane stared out the window of her cozy kitchen nook, gazing pensively at the limpid lake. The salty Breton breeze rippled the shimmery surface of *le Lac de Diane* as she prepared three mugs of sweet-smelling chamomile tea.

King Guillemin had taken the tart cherry and ginger tonic and was now resting comfortably in his private chambers, following a foot massage with healing oils administered by his attentive royal chamberlain Ezhvin.

Béatrice, *la Duchesse de Rohan*, had retired to her own guest room for a much-needed nap.

And, just as they had done weeks ago in this same cozy nook, the trinity of mothers now sat at Viviane's table, savoring a steaming mug of herbal *tisane*.

Tears of joy glimmering in her golden eyes, Laudine sighed happily. "My Yuletide wish has come true. All three of my sons are home for the holidays. And Bastien has married the woman he loves." She sipped her herbal tea and shook her head in disbelief. "He not only secured the safety of the Breton seas by defeating Ugolin le Clou and preserving *le Traîté Maritime…* but he will one day become the King of Finistère. I am so incredibly proud!" Auburn tresses highlighting her pretty face, a satisfied smile stretched from ear to ear.

"Gaston is absolutely overjoyed. It will be impossibly hard to let him go, but I couldn't ask for a better mentor than your son Lancelot." Ghislaine reached for Viviane's hand across the white linen topped table. "We'll get to see him every summer. Perhaps sometimes at Christmas, too." Tears spilled down her rosy cheeks, but she quickly whisked them away.

"Lancelot loves Gaston like a son. It makes my heart glad to see his joy." Viviane sipped her tea, the sweet chamomile lingering on her tongue as she smiled at her two closest friends. "This holiday season, we have all been truly blessed." She set her cup down, taking hold of her two friends' hands with a grateful smile. "The three of us each wished for our sons' happiness."

She closed her eyes in gratitude, giving them both an affectionate squeeze. "All of our Yuletide wishes have come true."

And sipping her chamomile tea, smiling at the mistletoe and boughs of evergreen, looking forward to the twelve days of Christmas with loving family and dear friends, Viviane exclaimed, her heart overflowing with love and holiday cheer, "This has indeed been the most wondrous winter solstice the Crystal Castle has ever seen."

A word about the author…

Jennifer Ivy Walker has an MA in French literature and is a professor of French at a state college in Florida. Her trilogy, “The Wild Rose and the Sea Raven”, is a paranormal romance fantasy adaptation of the medieval French legend of “Tristan et Yseult”, interwoven with elements of Arthurian myth, dark fairy tales, and haunting folklore from the enchanted Forest of Brocéliande.

Her newest novel, “Winter Solstice in the Crystal Castle”, is a passionate medieval romance between a fiery French Viking princess and the chivalrous knight who suffers an impossible love for her, ultimately winning the chance to compete for her coveted hand in marriage in the perilous Yuletide Joust.

Please visit the author here:

Website: https://jenniferivywalker.com/

Facebook:
https://www.facebook.com/JenniferIvyWalker

Twitter: https://twitter.com/bohemienneivy

Instagram:
https://www.instagram.com/jenniferivywalkerauthor/

Goodreads:
https://www.goodreads.com/author/show/22671046.Jennifer_Ivy_Walker

Bookbub:
https://www.bookbub.com/books/the-wild-rose-and-the-sea-raven-by-jennifer-ivy-walker

Thank you for purchasing
this publication of The Wild Rose Press, Inc.

For questions or more information
contact us at
info@thewildrosepress.com.

The Wild Rose Press, Inc.
www.thewildrosepress.com

Milton Keynes UK
Ingram Content Group UK Ltd.
UKHW012008080224
437493UK00013B/353

9 781509 251384